This book is for

my three 'kakis' — Ophelia Ooi, May Tsao & Helen Choo

my three boys — Chi-Min, Chi-Sharn & Shannan

my three cats — Mackerel, Zoe & Julius

Gift from the Gods

Suchen Christine Lim

Graham Brash, Singapore

First published in 1990 by
Graham Brash (Pte) Ltd
227 Rangoon Road
Singapore 0821

ISBN 9971-49-222-9

Reprinted 1991

Cover design by Hazel Yeo and Leong Wai Ying
Typeset by Linographic Services Pte Ltd
Printed in Singapore by C. W. Printing

Birth

How sad it is to be a woman;
Nothing is held so cheap.
Boys stand strong and firm,
Like gods fallen out of heaven.
No one is glad when a girl is born.

Hakka Cradle Song

Yenti's Journal

My father ran away to join the Communists in the Malaysian jungles the night I was born. I don't know him. The two or three times when I tried to find out more about him, Mother pursed her lips and remained silent. That was her way of telling me that that past in her life was dead. It had been willed out of existence.

1

The tropical thunderstorm had stopped as suddenly as it had begun, petering out into a light grey drizzle that fell continuously all afternoon. The dark trunk road, that ran from Taiping to Ipoh, cut through the plantations of straight rows of rubber trees, dripping with the wet. On the right of the village lay the railway, and on the left, the rubber plantations stretched as far as the eye could see, stopping abruptly at the edge of the tin mines and the slopes of the secondary jungle. Beyond this rose the mountains of the Main Range, jutting thousands of feet into the grey wet skies.

The farm lay at the edge of a plantation. Everything in the wooden farmhouse smelt damp because of the rain. Seventeen-year-old Pang Yoke-lin lay among the crumpled sheets of the four-poster bed, moaning softly.

A thin frail-looking girl, her face was bathed in sweat. The child inside her was due, and yet it was reluctant to emerge. She could feel it struggling and straining inside her, no longer a part of her, but something foreign with a will of its own. Her muscles were becoming tighter, and more and more taut with each new cycle of pain. The veins in her legs were swelling with the strain and she bit her lips as yet another wave of pain ripped through her pelvic region.

"Stop crying and push. Push!" First Aunt hissed in her ear.

Yoke-lin was breathing hard. She wanted to push the life out of her womb - get rid of it and hurl it into the laps of the Chows! She pushed and pushed at the urging of First Aunt till all that was loving, tender and affectionate was forced out of her heart.

Night came. From her bed in that tiny bedroom of

the farmhouse, Yoke-lin saw the hard profile of her mother-in-law. The coarse hands of the farm woman were lighting a pair of red candles on the altar of her Hakka ancestors. Softly intoning their names, she called their spirits home to witness the birth of the family's first grandchild.

The father-in-law, Old Chow, his weather-beaten face creased with worry, silently took down the kerosene lamp he reserved for festive occasions. He was concerned over the unusually long labour. Why was his grandson so reluctant to be born? Unconcerned about the mother, he feared that the long hours of strain might harm the baby.

He lit the lamp and pumped it till the room was bright as daylight. It was a good omen, and a good thing too that he had bought the lamp. The village was newly established by the British forces, and it had no electricity yet. "Government people, phui!" he spat, dismissing the officials' promise of a better life in these well-guarded New Villages established under the Emergency. What had that got to do with him? He was a farmer. All he wanted was to be left in peace to grow his crops and rear his fowl.

He strode into his daughter-in-law's bedroom and hung the lamp from a beam of the ceiling. Then he closed the room's only window, shutting out the black night. Like all peasants, he was superstitious - no one could tell what evil spirits might lurk out there, ready to harm the newborn.

The room was warm and bright. First Aunt bustled in, pushed Yoke-lin to one side of the bed and began lining it with cheap absorbent paper.

"The baby is due. I'll fetch the hot water."

Unable to bear her pain any longer, Yoke-lin let out a groan, then another and another, louder and louder. The pain in her loins was excruciating.

"Open your legs. Wider, ah! Wider!" her mother-in-law leant over her. "Hold your breath. Don't scream!"

"Remember, the medium said don't let out too much

air!" First Aunt cautioned her.

Yoke-lin gritted her teeth and tried not to make a sound, grasping the bed's headboard till her knuckles went white.

"I can see his head! Push, push!" First Aunt cried.

"Harder! Harder!" urged the mother-in-law. "He's coming!"

Yoke-lin obeyed with anger, frustration and despair.

"Aiya, where's Ah Chong? Has anyone looked for him? A father to be and he's not home yet!" the mother-in-law complained.

"You go, sister-in-law, you go. I'll look after her," said First Aunt.

Yoke-lin shut her eyes. She strained with all her strength like one pushing out her last breath, her soul and all the sinews of her heart, pushing out that part of her body which had been defiled. Soiled and defiled! Her eyes choked with angry tears. Cry after cry of rage escaped from her. She pushed until she thought her bones would crack. What did that man care? Night after night, he had shoved her on to the bed, planted his seed and left. He did what his father ordered him to do and that was that!

In their old age, fearing the end of their line, Old Chow and his wife had wanted a grandchild quickly. But their only child, Ah Chong, was more interested in "playing politics" than in marriage, the villagers said. Old Chow, a violent man, had had to box his ears on the wedding night.

"Go in and do it!" Old Chow had roared. "I paid two hundred for her, you know or not! I want a return. You hear me?"

The whole village heard him. For days afterwards, the villagers talked of nothing else but Ah Chong and his bride. "Have you done it?" the farmers guffawed.

The baby was coming. Yoke-lin could feel something tearing through her.

"Push, push!" Her mother-in-law held her legs.

"Push! With all your strength! Push!" First Aunt held her thrashing arms.

She was being torn apart. A long animal howl escaped from her as she shut her eyes and let the darkness slowly flood over her.

When she opened her eyes again, the room was bright and warm, the air damp with the smell of blood, and the papers under her were sodden wet. Pale and worn out, she could feel the sweat of labour flowing unchecked, soaking her sarong and the sheets beneath her. She lay back, exhausted.

"Aiya, no good, no good, a girl!" First Aunt was bending over her, looking distressed. The two of them stared at the pink bundle in her arms.

The father-in-law strode into the room. Without a word, he unhooked the kerosene lamp and extinguished it, plunging all of them into darkness.

Hours later, old Mrs Chow snuffed out the red candles, leaving only the oil lamp burning. The room was filled with shadows while outside, scattered dots of light showed the houses of the villagers. A warm breeze brought the foul smell of pigs' swill and manure. The heavy peasant woman let out a sigh and sat down on the earthen step of the doorway.

"It's fate. What else but fate," she muttered, trying to explain the incomprehensible to herself. "I did everything; saved the money for the bride, took her to the temple, made the son marry her and prayed to the ancestors, day and night."

"The girl's young. More grandchildren to come, maybe a son next year," First Aunt consoled her.

"Aiya, that's my prayer. My old mother had sons. No pain, no difficulty. They dropped out of her like piglets, ah.

Six boys, eight girls, one each year. All lived. Fifth Brother was born in the rice field. Ma bit off his cord with her own teeth! Born in the open, and yet he lived. But mine, they die! We Chows are cursed!"

"Choy! Choy!" First Aunt exclaimed. "Ah Chong will give you many grandsons yet. Where's Old Chow?"

"Gone to look for Ah Chong."

"The guards are so strict, they won't open the gates so late."

"I could see from his face," Mrs Chow continued, "Ah Chong's father was bitter. I thought he was going to slap Yoke-lin!"

"A girl! In my village in China they threw girls into the river," said First Aunt.

"In our village, Ma said that the fathers pressed their girl babies into the mud!"

And in her bedroom, Yoke-lin was sobbing quietly. She was a failure. During her twelve months in this Hakka household, the man who gave her this child had come and gone without a word. Sometimes, he was gone for days, and his mother would scold and blame her, saying she was a useless piece of wood, unable to hold on to the man she had married. What could she do? They never spoke. He came to her only when he was drunk. The few times that he had shown any interest in her, she was already big and clumsy with child, and he merely gave her some extra food to eat. Most of the time, they were strangers, doing what they had to.

But their child now lay sleeping by her side, the pink little face puckering up in tiny wrinkles. She had thought that this marriage would free her from being trapped in a fate like her mother's. Her mother - poor, illiterate, ignorant and stupid had lived with one man after another, dragging her brood of girls from small town to small town: Kulim, Bukit Mertajam, Batu Gajah, Telok Anson, an endless drabness in dim wooden huts upon which the rains pelted mercilessly and water dripped into rusty tins. Always on the move, always poor and in debt, never knowing when someone would buy them a meal, she grew up believing that a proper marriage was security.

Outside her bedroom the two older women were still whispering, their voices low and anxious as they waited for their menfolk to return. With the Emergency curfew it was not safe to walk about at night.

First Aunt came into the room. "Sleep," she ordered Yoke-lin. "After labour must rest. Boy or girl, you rest."

Yoke-lin's eyes filled with tears at this bit of kindness. Her own mother had not been so lucky. The trishaw rider with whom she had lived for many years had killed her when she gave birth to her sixth daughter. His face red with drink, he had raged like a mad bull because the baby was not the son he expected. He pulled her mother by the hair and dragged the still bleeding woman from her bed, slapping and punching her. Something was wrong with her body that could not produce a son. Again and again, he banged her head against the wall. His ancestors' graves were cold and it was her fault. Finally, her mother had collapsed. The children huddled under the table, wailing. That night, the sounds of pain from that tormented, writhing body on the floor had bewildered them. By morning their mother had bled to death. Yoke-lin, at the age of eight, became an orphan.

The baby on the bed let out a lusty wail. Yoke-lin awoke with a start and gathered her baby daughter into her arms. The farmhouse seemed full of angry people speaking in loud staccato Hakka.

"The fool! He's already dead!" Old Chow's voice rose above the din. "Let the horse-face guards shoot him! I have no son!"

"Choy! Choy! How can? Your one and only son!" the women gasped.

"What d'you want me do, ha? If not the soldiers now, it'll be the communists later! You think once inside, they'll let him come back to us?" Old Chow asked, exasperated by the events.

"Heaven, hear me, a poor mother! What wrong did I do that you punish me like this? I kowtow from temple to temple, and still I suffer like this?"

Old Mrs Chow knocked her head on the altar so violently that the ancestral tablets rattled.

"Sister-in-law, Ah Chong's mother, don't cry so. Not your fault. No one said you did wrong." First Aunt's voice rose and fell as more and more relations crowded into the farmhouse to have their say. Because all were from the same clan, the same village, or related by marriage, each felt he had a right to comment and advise the Chows on what to do. This was a family matter. A crisis had occurred, and the family must come together, to talk things over, to confer and decide on the best course of action to take. Such things, however, often lead to the teeth biting the tongue, as the old Chinese used to say, for no matter how close the family, members are bound to argue and quarrel at such times.

"If a son does wrong, a mother, what can she do? I don't have to be a god. I have eyes to see. I know Ah Chong's father blames me in his heart!" Mrs Chow raised her voice to clear herself from blame. "Why me? My fault that we've only one son ah? My womb bore him three sons! Remember, you aunts and uncles, three sons I bore him!"

"Sister-in-law, sister-in-law, peace, peace," an old uncle said. "We remember."

"Uncle, let me say this," she continued. "Why he blames me? Why not blame the war? Why not blame the Japanese soldiers? They killed his two sons! And why not fate? I blame my fate. Ill-fate! Did Ah Chong listen to me?

Ah Chong, I said, don't play with fire. This politics is fire! It burns! You all heard me. I cry, I scold, but who listens to his mother in times like these?"

"Oi! What for cry?" Old Chow's younger brother asked. "The bird has flown! Heads will roll! You can all be sure of it. Ha! Cry now, what for?"

Anger and fear, mixed with scorn for his wailing sister-in-law, were unmistakable in his loud voice. Like many relatives gathered there, he had grown-up sons, young farmers who could be unjustly implicated by Ah Chong's treachery and suffer at the hands of the authorities. Under the Emergency laws, anyone found helping the communists would be jailed or deported. It was bad enough that Chinese farmers like them had to live in villages fenced in by barbed wire, without one of their own kind bringing trouble upon their heads.

"Brother-in-law, Ah Chong brings trouble, I know," Mrs Chow cried. "I, his mother, bear the blame, the shame. Blame me, blame me!" She beat her chest. "I'd die first before your sons are harmed! My son, it's my son who has run into the jungle!"

"Shut your mouth, Ah Chong's mother! You spoiled the boy!" Old Chow's calloused hand banged on the table. His dark sun-burnt face was taut with the effort to control himself. Across his forehead the harsh lines deepened into the frown of a man frustrated by life's misfortunes.

"Dry your tears, Ah Chong's mother! No more tears, ah!" he shouted. "I shall tell the government people, no son, I have no son! Do what they like with his body! Shoot him! Kill him! I and my brothers ... aah, they have sons! All Chows! They can have my farm!"

At this, Mrs Chow broke out into a loud wail like a pig being slaughtered, weeping and snivelling in turns till her voice was hoarse with grief. This was the farm for which she had toiled all her life. How could her husband do this to her? How could her son leave her to such grasping relations? They, the Hakka farmers, had always clung to the land. But how could she if she had no son to inherit the land? For what purpose had been her life then? For what? The gods had promised her a grandson. Why hadn't her son waited? What had pulled him away from duty and home?

Mrs Chow's leathery face looked bewildered. No one could give her an answer. At this time, many peasant women were losing their sons to the war in the jungle. They too could not understand their young sons. The family had always been the centre of their world; how could they comprehend even one-tenth of the magnetic pull of the Chinese Communist slogans: Nation Before Self! No Nation, No Home! All that old Mrs Chow understood was that once her son had joined the communists, he was as good as dead. He would never be allowed to return to his family.

In her room, Yoke-lin was listening as the tears streamed down her face. Once again, it seemed, she had been abandoned. Her baby daughter, hungry and fretful, let out a thin wail.

"Stop the piglet's cry!" her father-in-law yelled. "No crying under my roof! I am not dead yet! Stop the tears! Change the luck! Get that broomstick spirit out of my house! Nothing but bad luck since she came! Out! Mother and daughter out! You hear me in there! Out!"

2

Tai Ku walked with the ambling gait of generations of Cantonese peasant women used to covering miles of country lanes between their villages and the wet rice fields. In her youth, she had been as tall as a Shantung horse, with large hands and large feet, a strong and useful helpmate who could toil beside her man in the rice fields.

But at the age of sixteen, during the year of the great famine, she was sold to a ship's captain who took her to the Nanyang, actually the Peninsula of Malaya, where she was sold to a brothel-keeper in the small town of Tapah. Now, a little stooped and wrinkled at forty-eight, she lived with her common-law husband of many years, Tai Shook the butcher, and their adopted daughter, Ah Jen.

If Tai Ku seldom mentioned her past, it was because she preferred to see herself as a devoted mother. And ever since a month ago when Yoke-lin, her other adopted daughter, had returned home with a baby girl, she had relished her grandmotherly role too. From within the dimness of her illiterate mind, the primordial values of generations of Han Chinese had sprouted roots, and Tai Ku, without quite knowing why, recognised that age was more respected than youth, and the grandmother, by virtue of her age, was given more respect than mothers or daughters. And so, by some circuitous reasoning, she concluded that having a grandchild, even though a worthless girl, was not such a bad thing if it raised her own status and others' regard for her.

So after one month, Tai Ku, the maternal grandmother, was celebrating the baby girl's First Moon with a chicken from the market and fifty eggs which must be boiled and dyed red before she distributed them to her neighbours in the tenement house. Though poor, she wanted to do everything properly according to tradition, and as she told her fellow tenant, Ah Por, she, Tai Ku, might have married a poor man but she knew what was right and proper. The Chow family would be given no cause for looking down on her. No one could say that she had forced her adopted daughter into an unfortunate marriage and then abandoned her. Who could have known that the Chows' son would bolt off like that? But "Hakkas are Hakkas and can't be trusted," she comforted herself with a saying which reflected the prejudice of her Cantonese ancestors who had fought the Hakkas for generations over the tin mines in Perak's rich Kinta Valley.

Tai Ku hurried down the narrow lane lined with make-shift wooden stalls, crammed with bundles of red candles, joss sticks and joss papers, paper clothes and paper shoes for the departed.

"Fifteenth of the month! Good luck, ah! Good luck day! Buy flowers for the gods!"

Street urchins screeched and flew around like mynah birds; trishaw men rang their bells to attract passengers; a woman shouted at the urchin who had pushed her off the pavement. Tai Ku jostled her way through the crowd. Her well-oiled chignon sat at the back of her head gleaming, held firmly in place by a jade hair pin and a gold ear-digger.

This latter ornament had a tiny scoop for digging the wax out of the ears and, at the other end, a sharp point for testing the tenderness of meat, and in the bedroom at night, for stabbing the exploratory hands of Tai Shook should they stray unbecomingly over unsanctioned parts of her person. After more than two decades of being his common-law wife, she felt she had given the man his due, and it was time now to put such unseemly behaviour behind them.

"Aaah, Tai Ku, sit down, sit down! A good morning to you!" Leong Sok, the letter writer, greeted her. "Very crowded this morning, feast of the gods."

"Ah Leong Sok, you read this for me." Tai Ku handed him a letter from her sworn-sister, Yee Mah, as she sat down on the stool placed near the writing table on the sidewalk.

Bent like an aged tortoise, Leong Sok adjusted the gold-rimmed glasses on the bridge of his nose, and spread out the letter on the table. He was an old bachelor who belonged to that brigade of pedantic scholars on the brink of poverty, the China letter writers who wrote and read the letters of thousands of illiterate immigrants and kept them in touch with their homeland while they toiled on foreign soil.

The simple implements of his trade were arrayed on one side of the table: Chinese paint brushes of various sizes in a porcelain jar, and an ink slab in a chocolate tin. There was also a small statue of the Goddess of Mercy with an urn of joss sticks in front of it, for Leong Sok was also a fortune-teller and an interpreter of the Chinese Almanac and Book of Change. As the wise man says, the man who can write his name is a scholar among the illiterate, and were it not for the general poverty of his clientele, the hand that held those brushes and painted the Chinese characters with such flourish could have commanded a higher fee and lived a more comfortable life.

"Ahem!" he cleared his throat, "I see it is from your sister, Yee Mah."

"That's right. What does she say?" Tai Ku asked eagerly.

"Let me see, let me see," and there was a long pause before he finally said, "She asks after your good health, and that of your family. She says she hopes ..."

"Aiya, Ah Leong Sok, go on, go on! Every letter begins in the same way, mah! I know that!"

"Be patient, Tai Ku!" He was used to her lack of patience. But, as he laboriously explained to her, it was his duty to convey every word in the letter.

"What does my sister say?" Tai Ku asked again.

"She says she's writing to let you know that she's coming to Ipoh, next month," Leong Shook read out. "She says it's time to change the family's luck, time to go to the temple. A medium at Anson, very powerful, serving the Ninth Lord of the Heavens."

"Then she has received the letter I asked you to write last month?" Tai Ku asked.

"Aaah, let me see - eyes not so good now." He searched the page of flowery characters. "Ah, here it is! She says, I have received your respectful letter. We will talk when I come. And, and further down, she says, Ah Kiong never listens to me. He still sleeps on his single bed, and Siew Lai is very unhappy."

"What can a mother do? These young masters always want their own way; never listen! Aiya, the shame and sorrows of families!" Tai Ku shook her head and thought of Yoke-lin, the married daughter who had been sent home.

"These young ones, not like us," Leong Sok clucked sympathetically; it was something that he did, often without thought, whenever he read such letters to customers.

"What can a mother do, you tell me? You plan and plan, but fate is fate! Is that a mother's fault?"

"I know, I know, Tai Ku. Your sister slaves for her son," Leong Sok said.

"Who can say I don't slave for my daughters?"

"No one, no one, Tai Ku!" the letter writer protested immediately.

"I slave for my daughters! True, true, the two are not my flesh and blood, but who can accuse me of not being a mother to them? All these years? Which mother, you tell me, Ah Leong Sok, which mother doesn't want her daughter to marry well? They marry well, I am well. They marry poor, I am poor, right or not? I'm not so heartless as to want my daughters to marry poor!"

"No, no, Tai Ku, I've known you all these years; you come to me and I write your letters. Aaah, I know you, Tai Ku," the letter writer assured her.

"Ah Leong Sok, you're most kind." Tai Ku beamed and lowering her voice a little, she continued, "Other people at my tenement house, not so kind. Whisper behind my back, say I forced Yoke-lin into it! Not to my face, no, they wouldn't dare, but behind my back they talk, and heaven can't close their mouths! They say I take the money and marry her to a good-for-nothing!"

"Not true! Nonsense, nonsense!" Leong Sok exclaimed.

"You have eyes! Can see for yourself, Ah Leong Sok. When Yoke-lin married, I brought you cakes only, right or not? I couldn't even afford a piece of roast pork for you!"

"Small matter, small matter, Tai Ku," he murmured.

But the letter writer would have loved a piece of roast pork, and his mouth watered at the thought of munching succulent meat with his bowl of rice.

"Aiya..." he gave a little sigh. "To tell the truth, I haven't eaten roast pork for months, Tai Ku. Too, too expensive for a poor letter writer like me. But you're different. The wife of a butcher can eat pork everyday."

"True, true, it was I who arranged the match," Tai Ku continued single-mindedly, deliberately ignoring the letter-writer's outrageous hint. She was not in the habit of giving away good pork just because she happened to be the butcher's wife. "And so ... I asked Old Chow about the dowry. My daughter is a good girl, I said. She can cook, and she can sew. Only one hundred dollars he offered me. What! One hundred! I said to him. I looked after the girl and paid for everything she has, and you give me a hundred? Not even enough to pay for her clothes!"

Even the memory made Tai Ku indignant. "These Hakkas!" She shook her head. "You give them one inch, they want one yard. Like squeezing water out of a stone!

Then at last, he paid two hundred."

"Hmmm, good sum, good sum, Tai Ku," murmured the letter-writer. "Mrs Ching next door asked for fifty dollars only, a small red packet. Not the kind to sell off her daughter, she said. Told me herself. A very wise woman, that Mrs Ching."

The letter-writer's barb was deliberately sharp since Tai Ku had so uncharitably ignored his hint for a small slice of pork.

"The gods know I spend money on my daughters, Ah Leong Sok! I, Tai Ku, am not like other mothers! Dress myself in fine clothes and let my daughters go in rags! Mrs Ching is a lucky woman! She has a son. I've only daughters. If I don't get something now, ah, who do I depend on next time? Must save for old age, right or not?" Tai Ku spoke with animation; she had to convince Leong Sok that she had done nothing improper in asking for a bigger dowry. "Yoke-lin's mother, if she were alive today, she would have done the same, mah! Money is money. Not that I'm money-faced, but you and I, Ah Leong Sok, we've been through a war. Japanese time, no food to eat. No one in this world gives you food if you've no money! Who will ever bring coal to a poor man in winter? A fat purse is better than an empty stomach, right or not?"

"But you're not poor now, Tai Ku. I am poor, but not you, not you," Leong Sok replied as his eyes darted to the basket at her feet. "Who doesn't know that the butcher's wife eats pork everyday? We poor letter-writers are no better than beggars." He shook his head regretfully. "Can only eat pork if others are generous."

"Aiya, Ah Leong Sok, you flatter me truly. I'm not a rich woman. Today is my granddaughter's first moon. This roast pork is for the gods!"

Nevertheless, anxious to retain the goodwill of the letter writer, Tai Ku handed him a small slice.

"Thank you, thank you, Tai Ku! Many thanks! A

poor man does not refuse." Smirking, the old man quickly wrapped the slice of meat in a scrap of newspaper and shoved it into his grubby bag. "I always say you have a kind heart, Tai Ku."

3

Two rows of pre-war Chinese shophouses, built in the early nineteen hundreds, lined Ming Sun Lane. With thick brick walls, these solid two-storeyed buildings were shops on the ground floor and tenement cubicles for poor families on the upper floor. Large families with many mouths to feed - father, mother, five or six children, and a grandparent or two - lived cramped into one tiny cubicle. Those who could afford it crowded into cubicles with windows, and those who could not afford the higher rent sweated at night in windowless rooms. Those even poorer still, like retired coolies and trishaw riders, rented bunk space under the stairways or along the dank corridors, lit only by a skylight in the roof.

Tai Ku's cubicle above the grocer's in Ming Sun Lane cost her thirty dollars a month. But it was the largest cubicle in the tenement house with a window facing the main road instead of the back lane; and she had the respect of her landlord, the grocer. She was the only tenant who paid her rent regularly and promptly, but that, in Tai Ku's mind, had everything to do with her own peerless thrift and sense of dignity, not Tai Shook's timely handing over of the household allowance each month.

Her cubicle was scrupulously clean for Tai Ku hated dust and dirt. Poverty had nothing to do with dirt, she used to say. The floor was mopped and the furniture was dusted every day. She was the proud owner of a brass bed and mattress, gifts from her first husband, the tin miner who had bought her from the brothel in Tapah where she was known as "Ah Fah" the Flower. But having been deflowered years ago by the landlord of her father's farm, this name had lost its significance and was best forgotten now that she was known as the butcher's wife.

It could not be said that she was proud of her status, she who had seen better days when she was living with the miner. He had bought her a son for the then princely sum of three hundred dollars, and had adopted a daughter, Ah Jen, as well. "Aaah, your Tai Ku had certainly come down upon this world," she sighed to her sworn-sister, Yee Mah, who was fortunate enough to have married an old man who had left her a goldsmith shop. She, Tai Ku, was less fortunate and had suffered terrible things.

As fate would have it, her son, a weak little two year old to begin with, had choked on a fish bone and died of septic poisoning when Tai Ku took the boy to a temple medium instead of a doctor. To this day, however, she would grit her teeth whenever the subject was brought up, and argue vehemently with anyone who dared to blame the medium for her son's death. Her own ill fate did it was all she said, and she was destined to die without any son to mourn her passing.

As she walked down the lane, a skinny boy came running. "Tai Ku! Tai Ku!" he called out. He was a tough-looking ten year old, brown from the sun, with scabs of old sores covering his bare arms and legs.

"Look! I've caught another one!" The urchin proudly pointed to a rat in the wire cage held in his hand. The black vermin, the size of a small kitten, was scampering round and round its rusty prison.

"Where did you catch it?" Tai Ku asked.

"In your coal box, next to the firewood."

"Must be the bits of food dropped from the wok. It went after the food."

"I'll kill it," the boy declared and waited with an expectant look in his eyes.

"Nah, here's your five cents." Tai Ku handed him the coin.

"Thank you, Tai Ku!"

The young rat-catcher sped off to join his companions in the back lane. Tai Ku lugged her basket and followed.

Hoots of jubilant laughter greeted the urchin and his prized catch. The boys and girls, with little brothers and sisters in tow, gathered round the wire cage. An eight-year-old ruffian pushed the others aside and poured half a bottle of kerosene on the black rat. Then another one, eyes glinting with malice, lit a match and flung it into the cage. Instantly, the rat was engulfed in a ball of flames. Shrill screams filled the air as the tortured creature raced round and round, senselessly hitting itself against the sides of the cage. The little girls shrieked and clung to one another, horrified and yet drawn towards the gruesome sight. The boys whooped and yelled, hopping first on one foot and then on the other, drunk with their own cruelty. Then another urchin swaggered towards the flaming cage, paused, and after looking around him, pulled down his ragged pants and directed a trajectory of yellow pee on to the flames. Hiss and smoke, boos and cheers accompanied his act. Finally, one of the urchins flung the sodden carcass into the nearby drain, and the circus of cruelty came to an end.

Tai Ku, who had been watching all this while, turned and climbed the stairs with the righteousness of a hanging judge who has meted out well-deserved punishment. If she could not be rich like her sworn-sister, she would at least be as clean and rid her cubicle and kitchen of those vermin.

The upper storey of the grocer's tenement house was usually quiet in the morning. Only the women remained in the hot airless cubicles or in the communal kitchen where everyone crowded in to cook, wash, bathe, or sit around and gossip. The communal kitchen used to be a balcony for the daughters of a rich trader, so that they could enjoy the cool evening breeze without leaving the seclusion of their family quarters. Now covered with a zinc roof, it had a row of brick stoves at one end and in the corner of the other end was the communal bathroom, a two-by-two foot cubicle, partitioned off by four sheets of zinc which did not quite reach the floor. Those cooking in the kitchen could see the legs of anyone bathing inside, so, out of modesty, the women usually bathed during the day and the menfolk at night, after the evening meal.

Tai Ku's brass bed, wardrobe and some cheap wooden shelves filled one side of her cubicle. A round table used for all meals, four or five stools, a sewing machine and a small cupboard, which served as a larder, lined the other side of the rectangular room. What remained was a narrow passageway, just wide enough for two persons to lie down side by side. The matchwood-thin partitions separating the cubicles were covered with a yellowish wallpaper that was peeling in parts and infested with baby bugs which hid in the cracks of the planks. Tai Ku fought a perpetual battle with them but the bugs had an uncanny way of evading insecticide and boiling water. They were the bane of the poor, chewing up their wallpaper and cheap calendars.

Tai Ku, on reaching the landing, put down her heavy basket and stopped to catch her breath.

"Tai Ku, home from the market so early? What did you buy?" Ah Sow, wife of the noodle hawker, peered into her basket.

"Nothing much, just a chicken for praying. Look at this scrawny one!" Tai Ku held up the bird by its neck. "Forty-five cents today, not one cent less! Last week it was cheaper!"

"Wah, this skinny thing so expensive! And now not even new year yet!"

"It's all this moving to new villages, mah. Many farmers have to move, the vegetable man says."

"Right-lor! My old father and mother got to go too, far away. How to sell in the market here, you tell me?" Ah Sow seemed ready to stop and talk about her parents' woes.

But Tai Ku had more important things on her mind this morning than to indulge in idle chatter about the government's New Villages. The communists in the jungles, the army and the state of emergency were things unrelated to her except that now she and Tai Shook had to be careful about their Hakka son-in-law. She did not think it wise to criticise the New Villages and be suspected of sympathising with the communists. The troubles of those who farmed in the countryside did not concern her.

"Aiya, Ah Sow, no time to talk! Must boil all these eggs now! Fifty chicken eggs at thirty-five cents, and the man wouldn't let me choose!" Tai Ku exclaimed.

"Why so many eggs?" Ah Sow's mother-in-law, Ah Por, waddled up to them.

"Just some red eggs for my poor granddaughter. Born and nobody wants her! But still my granddaughter, mah! Let it not be said that I, Tai Ku, don't know my duty! Not my own flesh and blood, but I still treat her like my own," Tai Ku announced.

"Humph! We celebrate the birth of grandsons only! That's the way I was brought up." Ah Por sniffed at Tai Ku's apparent disregard for tradition. "Daughters! They marry and change their names!"

"Er, Tai Ku, about Yoke-lin," Ah Sow began, "was there -aiya, you know how people talk! Was there, er, no wrong doing on her part?" Ah Sow asked, sniggering a little at the audacity of her own question. "It's true? The Chows just threw her out?"

Like the rest of the tenants, Ah Sow had wondered about Yoke-lin's sudden reappearance with a baby girl in her arms. By the looks of it, she had whispered to her mother-in-law, Tai Ku and her daughter must be hiding something scandalous. There was more to it than met the eye. Men did not know and the spirits did not see, as the saying went, so who could tell what had gone wrong. The tenants whispered among themselves and finally agreed that Yoke-lin must have done something to sully the good name of the Chows. Why else would they have asked her to leave with the baby? The trishaw rider's wife, who lived downstairs, had rolled her eyes knowingly. Who could say, the baby might not even be a Chow, she had whispered. Had not the Chow family an only son? And he had run away! Why, old Mrs Chow had complained to a relative, who in turn had told the trishaw rider's wife herself, that if Yoke-lin had been more submissive, her son might have stayed.

"Ah Sow, you tell me, what wrong has my daughter done?" Tai Ku began. "What can I say? Like swallowing a dead cat, my mouth's stuffed! You tell me, what can a mother do? You slave to bring up your daughter! Not my flesh, but never mind! You make sure she's married well. Then what happens? She returns crying, a newborn babe in her arms! I've no more face to hide! You have the heart to throw mother and baby out? I, Tai Ku, am not like other mothers. I haven't!"

She was, however, angry all the same that Yoke-lin had brought dishonour and great loss of face to her, and yet she, Tai Ku, must not be seen to abandon her adopted daughter at a time like this. After all, everybody knew she had made this match for Yoke-lin.

"Tai Ku, I for one, ah, always say you have a soft heart! All these years, my old eyes have seen how well you treat your daughters. We all say your heart is good! You know our Ah Sow, very blunt with her mouth!" Ah Por soothed her. "Always she speaks first, think later!"

"Ah Por," Tai Ku replied, taking out a large white handkerchief to dab the corners of her eyes, "you know me, Ah Por. What have I done to deserve this shame? Have I not suffered enough? I had hoped - don't all mothers hope? - I had hoped to marry her off. She's comfortable, I'm also comforted, right or not? How could I know - I'm not a god - how could I know that it would come to this?"

"Aiya, Tai Ku, no one is blaming you! How can we mothers know the hearts of our children? You and I, old friends. Between old friends, let me say this. Not that I want to cause trouble, but you know how people talk, chit-chit-chit!"

Tai Ku nodded, and Ah Por, a soft, fat, damp and cringing sort of woman, continued eagerly. She loved to talk and could gossip all day, repeating the same story over and over again to anyone who would listen. From her makeshift bed along the dark corridor, just outside her son's cubicle, she kept a close watch on the comings and goings of the tenants. Nothing escaped her beady eyes.

"A relation of the Chows says that Yoke-lin was not willing," reported Ah Por. "We all know what a young man wants! Hard for the woman! But if you're married, you're married, and must give what a man wants. Life's like that. The Chows called her a block of wood! Never a smile on her face, they said. Who could blame their son for running away?"

"Always they blame the woman first!" Ah Sow exclaimed, full of indignation. "If the baby had been a boy, you think Yoke-lin would have been kicked out? They would have treated her like a queen, even if their son had run away! And that's the truth!"

Ah Sow walked away, having driven this point home to her mother-in-law. Earlier on, before the birth of her grandson, Ah Por had made many derisive remarks about her daughter-in-law when four granddaughters had been born, one after the other. There was something wrong with her daughter-in-law's womb, she had insinuated. She had even pestered her hawker son to take another wife so that his mother, Ah Por, could have a grandson to mourn her death. Only poverty and the birth of the fifth child, a boy, had saved Ah Sow from being cast aside, and she had never quite forgiven the mother-in-law's devious attempts to loosen the marital bond, however tenuous, between husband and wife. "Mothers-in-law, ha! They only have eyes for the male that drops out of you!" Ah Sow huffed.

"Right-lor, right! Talk back at me now! Act like a queen! Ingrate! If not for my praying, you think you have a son today?" Ah Por screeched.

"Aiya, let her be! Save your breath to warm your stomach!" Tai Ku soothed her. "Young women, all like this!"

"Look at her, Tai Ku! Just look at her! Don't say I complain all the time, ah! Do I ask her to serve me tea in the morning and rice in the evening? I help look after the children. I don't sit like an old Buddha and do nothing! Where else can she find a mother-in-law like me? Not that I want to praise myself!"

"True, true! In this life, we mothers bear all the pain," responded Tai Ku automatically before reverting to a more immediate grievance. "Now just look at these eggs. Thirty-five cents! This chicken? Forty-five! And this roast pork, three dollars! Every day in confinement, steamed liver, steamed pork, chicken in white wine. I spend money like water, but who knows? You think that Tai Shook gives me extra, ah? Thunder will have to strike that butcher before he opens his fist and gives me another cent!" Tai Ku patted Ah Por's shoulders lightly. "We all have our problems! You see my outside good, I see your outside good! But only good to see, not good to eat!"

"But, Tai Ku, surely your daughter will work next time and pay you back?" Ah Por asked.

"Aiya, I daren't hope! What can she do? Serve in that coffee stall again? Not even enough to feed herself!"

"Then why spend so much on the baby? Just a girl!"

"Those Chows are Hakkas. We Cantonese have more feelings. No grandchild of mine shall come into this world poor and shabby! I might be poor but I have back bone! I will not let those Chows look down on me," Tai Ku declared. "Let them remember, ah, and I don't care who tells them "- she raised her voice -"I have relations who own a goldsmith shop! I brought up Yoke-lin and I will bring up this baby too! Let the gods open their eyes and the heavens hear!"

Tai Ku's voice could be heard throughout the tenement house, and once again everyone heard how her mercy and charity had known no bounds when Yoke-lin's mother had died leaving a starving brood behind, and how she, Tai Ku, had even pawned her gold necklace to redeem the poor child from the brothel to which she had been sold by that brute of a step-father.

"I didn't count the cost," Tai Ku declared. "When I help, I help all the way. You want to accompany the Lord Buddha, accompany him all the way, I always say."

"Right, so right, Tai Ku! In this house, who doesn't know your good heart?" Ah Por said ingratiatingly, her lips curling into a smile that belied the smoothness of her voice.

But, Tai Ku, too wrapped up in recounting her own virtues, could only shake her head deprecatingly. She lugged her basket into the kitchen where she promptly cut a large slice of the roast pork and presented it to Ah Por amidst the profusion of refusals and thanks which is common among polite hypocrites.

4

Inside the cubicle, Yoke-lin wiped away a tear and cradled her infant daughter in her arms, gently stroking the tuft of hair, soft as down. She wished Tai Ku could understand how it pained her to hear all that about her past. What was past was past, and all she wanted now was to put her year with the Chows behind her and begin anew. She still had the resilience of youth, though neither grief nor elation moved her these days. Her heart seemed frozen, except for one tiny corner into which the newborn babe had stolen during the past confinement month.

Fervently, she had wished for a son, and not this puny girl. But then, there it lay in her arms, bald and pink, tugging at her heart as if the navel cord which had connected its frail little body with hers had not been broken. The baby yawned, her open mouth like a small black hole, her face puckering up like a wizened old lady's. Yoke-lin hugged her close, pressing her baby against her breast, the baby girl no one wanted.

She resolved to return to work as soon as she could, any work as long as it would sustain her daughter and herself. Working for her own living was nothing new. She had had a very short childhood. At twelve, she had been sent out by Tai Ku to wash dishes and wait at tables, working from eleven in the morning to eleven each night. During the Japanese Occupation, when Tai Shook was without work, she had supported the whole family through her job at the rubber factory. At seventeen, when Tai Ku had asked her to marry Old Chow's son, she had agreed obediently, accepting as fate the decision of those whose charity she had depended on. But this baby girl was her own, her very own, and she would call her Yenti, the tears of a swallow. Her daughter would be the swallow which would soar above pain and sorrow. She would educate her so that she would be independent and free!

"Here, come, let me carry her," Tai Shook said as he entered the cubicle, and bending over the bed, scooped the baby into his arms.

He stood at the window with the baby, looking down at the children playing in the lane below. He was a short man, with a skin browned by the sun and a thin face etched with deep worry lines. Being half a head shorter than his wife, he was used to being bullied into silence by her, and usually kept his thoughts to himself. A sharp word from her was enough to send him into his shell for he disliked conflict and preferred peace to victory.

When he was eighteen, he had been kidnapped by a labour gang and shipped from his village in Canton to the Malay Peninsula. He had then been sold to a tin miner who worked him in the mines near Ipoh. But later, due to ill health, he had been unable to mine and had been re-sold to a butcher from whom he had learnt his trade. He had worked for the butcher for more than fifteen years, waking up every day at three in the morning to slaughter the pigs and never getting into bed till ten or eleven each night. Every day for fifteen years, it had been the same routine, without a break except for the three days during the Lunar New Year when all Chinese stopped work and closed shop.

When he was nearly forty, Tai Shook had saved enough money to buy his freedom and set himself up as a butcher, peddling pork from house to house in and around Ipoh, the town he had never left ever since his arrival from China. It was as if the fear and excitement, the pain and hardship of that single voyage across the South China Sea had been enough to last him a life time.

He had never been an ambitious man. All he asked of life was a home, three square meals a day, and some people he could call family. Years later, when he died, it was said that there was hardly enough money left to bury him. Tai Ku had spent it all.

"Has she had her milk?" he asked again.

Tai Shook asked Yoke-lin the same question every day. It was his way of showing concern for the baby girl. He seemed to be interested in her and nothing else. He did not ask Yoke-lin why she had returned, or why she had been thrown out of her in-laws' house. Such things did not seem to bother him. When she had come home, a month ago, he had neither welcomed her nor spoken to her. However, the next day, he had brought back pork and liver, and had been bringing back special cuts of meat throughout her month of confinement. Yoke-lin knew that the pork which Tai Ku had so liberally cooked and distributed among the tenants had come out of Tai Shook's meagre earnings each month.

"What will you call her?" Tai Shook asked.

"Ah Jen and I, we thought Yenti is a good name."

"Hmm, a name in Mandarin," he muttered, quite amazed, for he had an illiterate man's respect for that language of the Chinese scholars.

"The name sounds better in Mandarin than in Cantonese. Yen is swallow, and Ti means tears," Yoke-lin explained.

"A swallow that will soar above tears, Ah Pa," Ah Jen said, coming in with a basin of water.

She was a sturdy girl of fifteen who still wore her hair in a pony tail, tied with a rubber band. She was studying in a school run by some Christian missionaries and had learned a little about the outside world.

"Soong Mei-ling is a Mandarin name, and, she and her sisters, they went to America to study!"

"What are you all talking about? Chit-chit-chit like chickens in a coop! Time to pray! And time to shave this piglet's head. And give her a good name." Tai Ku bustled into the cubicle with a tray laden with a boiled chicken, a roast duck, a pig's tongue - for eloquence, she explained -

and oranges for good fortune. "Come, come, hand me the piglet! I'll shave off that bit of hair and bathe her. The gods have given her a name - Lan Fah."

"But, Ma, I thought I would -" Yoke-lin tried to protest.

"You people only think but I, the old cow here, do all the work! I went to the temple early-early this morning. The medium says, ah, this piglet will have a hard life next time. Call her Lan Fah, he said, name of a hardy flower. Grows by the roadside!"

"But, Ma, my teacher says," Ah Jen joined in, "only low class families give their daughters names of flowers. Women who sell their bodies are nearly always called Flower or Rose! Ah Fah or Mui Kwai!"

"Ah Jen! Young girls shouldn't have big mouths!" Tai Ku scolded her daughter. "Older folks talk, you listen! If you don't speak, no one will say you're dumb!"

"But, Ma, Yenti is a beautiful Mandarin name, very meaningful!" Ah Jen protested.

"You speak Cantonese! Cantonese must speak Cantonese! I send you to school to learn, not to come back and speak a different tongue to me!"

"Yenti means swallow, like a swallow flying high above, free of sorrow," Yoke-lin explained again.

"What kind of name is that?" Tai Ku scoffed. "Whoever, you tell me, whoever heard of tears or sorrow or sadness in a girl's name? The piglet's life is hard enough. You want her to cry all her life, ah? Give her a name like that?"

A thin wail rose from the baby, and Tai Ku snatched her out of Tai Shook's arms.

"Mad, all of you! Not an auspicious name!" Tai Ku held the baby's head over the basin of water and began to shave off the tuft of baby hair. The infant struggled and wailed. "There, there, my precious, you'll be a big girl after this!"

Yoke-lin, watching the hair shaving ritual, refused to

give in, however. Not this time. The child was hers; she had produced this baby. It was not someone's charity; it came from her.

The baby was crying again. "Don't cry, lor-lor, my piglet, don't cry. A little bit more and then you'll be nice and bald," Tai Ku crooned. "Aiya, you mad people! Yenti! Ha! As if she hadn't enough tears already! A bad name! A bad omen, I say!"

"But Ma, my wedding day was auspicious, and yet see what happened," Yoke-lin pointed out. "Auspicious or not, fate is fate! If it's fated, it'll happen, can't blame a name, can't even blame people."

It was hardly a criticism of herself but Tai Ku took it to heart. She looked up, her eyes furious, as she pointed an accusing finger at Yoke-lin seated on the bed.

"Ingrate! Blaming me for your marriage? I worked my heart out for you and this is what I get? If I'd known, I'd have let you slave till no one wanted you! Who thinks of you? Me! Who plans for you? Me! Who, I ask you, worries for you? Day and night, till my hair is white? Me, this old cow!"

There was no stopping her words or her volume once Tai Ku got started. She raged and fumed and scolded.

"You come home, thrown out by other people! Not a squeak from you! Did I say a word? Ha? Answer me! I only squeeze my own heart and suffer my shame in silence! Did I complain? No money, did I ask you?"

"Quietly, quietly," Tai Shook mumbled. "No need to shout so, the whole house can hear. Yoke-lin is not blaming you."

"Butcher, you keep quiet! What do you know? A poor butcher all your miserable life! Remember, she married at seventeen! I, ah, at fifteen! Who cared about me then? She at least has got me! Who, who did I have?"

"Ma, all right, Ma!" Ah Jen tried to calm her down.

"All the same, you people all the same! My fate to

have ingrates around me all my life! Nah! Take her back!" She thrust the baby into Yoke-lin's arms. "Call her what you like! Don't come to me, I'm only the grandmother!" Tai Ku stalked out of the room.

The baby was named Yenti, and eventually, Tai Ku accepted it after Yoke-lin had kowtowed and offered her tea to beg for forgiveness.

5

The following month, Tai Ku's sworn sister, Yee Mah, arrived from the island of Penang. In her chauffeur-driven Mercedes were her daughter-in-law, Siew Lai, and Ah Yoong, the black-and-white amah. The tenants of Ming Sun Lane were agog with excitement and curiosity. A Mercedes, much less a chauffeur-driven one, had never been parked in their lane.

The sworn sisters were as unlike each other as a withered peanut and a ripe round chestnut. Tai Ku was stooped and wrinkled, while the other was smooth and plump, with the well-fed look of those who enjoy a life of ease. Bending solicitously over Yee Mah and pouring her a cup of tea, Tai Ku looked much older than her forty-eight years, while her sister, at fifty, still had a comely face.

This business woman and owner of a goldsmith shop had permed her hair, discarded the usual cotton samfoo suits in favour of soft silk samfoo jackets worn over tailored pants and matching black court shoes. Attired like a rich Chinese trader's wife, she wore a band of gleaming jade on each wrist, a gold ring with seven diamonds set into a star on her left hand, and in her right she was holding a large gold watch with the thick gold chain twisted round her fingers. It had once belonged to her husband, the late Mr Chan Fook Seng, who had founded Prosperity Goldsmith; and looking at it now, Yee Mah observed to Tai Ku as she sipped her tea, that whatever the time might be by other people's clocks, it was gone past half-past eleven by Mr Chan's gold watch given to him by an English gwai-lo who had brought it all the way from his country, she announced to the rest of the company.

"Where's Tai Shook? Doesn't the butcher know, ah,

that at my shop we eat the mid-day meal at eleven-thirty? My health, you know Tai Ku, is not what it used to be! Eat every day at the same time, my doctor advised me. Don't eat like in your younger days, he says."

She turned to Ah Sow's mother-in-law, who was gazing at her, full of admiration for her wealth. "Aiya, Ah Por! You don't know me yet! I followed our Mr Chan, my late husband, everywhere, even into the jungle. Which woman dared, ah? Only me! What have I not seen!"

They were all listening to her: Yoke-lin nursing the baby on the bed, Ah Jen and Ah Por seated on the floor, and the other tenants who had stopped by the cubicle to stand and stare and listen to Yee Mah's tales of adventure during her gem-buying trips with her husband. All agreed that she was a well-travelled and knowledgeable lady although in actual fact, she had only been as far north as Kedah and as far south as Selangor, never once leaving the Malay Peninsula.

"Tai Ku, where is your butcher?" Yee Mah asked again, looking repeatedly at her precious watch.

"Don't wait, don't wait! We eat first," Tai Ku assured her. "I don't know where the butcher has gone."

"No, no, we wait. I might be rich, but I don't expect others to change their times to suit me, you know," said Yee Mah, forgetting her earlier pronouncement.

"Eat now, the soup's hot and ready. I got up early-early this morning to boil it for hours so it'll be ready when you come."

"Why so much trouble?" Yee Mah patted her sister's work-worn hand. "All relations here, one family, mah! Next time don't go to so much trouble."

"No, no, sister, no trouble!" Tai Ku was beaming at this acknowledgement of family ties in front of so many tenants, ties bonding her to the goldsmith shop in Penang, the glitter of the diamond ring, the gleaming jade and the status of having a black-and-white amah and a Malay chauffeur. "Aiya, so good you come! Family is family, I know, but still, first time you come, so I must cook something special for you. But what does Siew Lai like?"

"Our Siew Lai is very delicate," Yee Mah replied. "I don't have to tell you, she's from a very rich family. Richer than me! Ah Yoong here looks after her."

Siew Lai, only a year older than Yoke-lin, was sitting like an equal with the elderly women at the round table. Her bulging goldfish eyes surveyed the cubicle with scorn. Disdainfully she held a handkerchief to her nose as if the odour of the room and its occupants offended her delicate olfactory nerves. Tai Ku, glancing at the girl, pursed her lips but she refrained from saying anything.

"Ah Yoong, so hot here!" Siew Lai said peevishly.

Yee Mah's daughter-in-law was not only rude, Yoke-lin observed, but she was also ugly, with short arms, short legs and a tubby figure which was quite incongruent with her affected delicacy and weak constitution. A duck pretending to be a swan, Tai Ku would have said if she had not had to watch her words and be polite to her honoured guests.

"Ah Yoong, this room is so hot! Please fan me. Not enough air," Siew Lai complained again.

The amah produced a beautiful pink goose feather fan such as those used on the stage, and started fanning her young mistress. The urchins and their mothers standing just outside the cubicle doorway gaped and gawked at the sight.

"Ya, very stuffy this room, Tai Ku," echoed Yee Mah, thoroughly enjoying the attention her daughter-in-law was getting. "Our Siew Lai here is not used to the heat. Must always have an electric fan. And now, with a granddaughter, time for you to get a bigger room."

"Aiya, Yee Mah, not that I don't want a bigger room! Who, tell me, who doesn't? But my purse is too small," Tai Ku replied.

"At your age, I hope you're not supporting two daughters and a granddaughter as well!" Yee Mah exclaimed.

"But what can Yoke-lin do now? There's the baby, and, ah, such things must come from the heart. Other people will say I forced her, turned her out to work, lived off her earnings! Not my flesh and blood, very difficult," Tai Ku said, her barbed words meant for Yoke-lin's ears.

"Chieh! What nonsense! Not your flesh, right, but still you're the mother! All these years, you looked after her! Time enough to pay the debt, and show some gratitude, ah, Yoke-lin?" Yee Mah turned to her.

"Yee Mah, I know my duty. I will work and support all of them. I've not forgotten my debt," Yoke-lin declared, angry that her aunt and mother should choose to discuss her want of gratitude in front of so many people, trying to shame her by doing so.

"You speak from your heart?" Yee Mah asked.

"I speak as I think! I say it, I will do it!" Yoke-lin replied.

"Good, good! Your Yee Mah here is happy! Put flesh into those brave words!"

By that time, lunch was over, and as there was still no sign of Tai Shook, Ah Jen was ordered to clear the table. Siew Lai, complaining of a headache, left for the hotel with Ah Yoong in attendance.

The two sisters settled down to enjoy a quiet smoke on the floor. Now that her wealthy daughter-in-law had left, Yee Mah could relax, sitting cross-legged on the mat, relishing the prospect of a home-made cigarette such as those smoked by peasant women in China. This was their bond. Both were peasant women sold over the Nanyang to become prostitutes. Tai Ku, hunched over a pillow tucked against her abdomen, was rolling a cigarette, packing the raw tobacco firmly with a practised hand while Yee Mah waited contentedly. The air in the room was warm for the cubicle's only window was shut to keep out the afternoon sun. When both women had lit up, they began to talk, slowly, languidly, inhaling the pungent nicotine.

"Tell me, why are you taking Ah Siew Lai to the temple of the Ninth Lord of the Heavens?" Tai Ku asked.

"Tai Ku, now we're alone, I can tell you. What else can I do? One year already and still no child! No, coming to two years already! And Ah Kiong, the rascal, always not home! In and out of the house, never stay the night, never talk to Siew Lai. So what to do? She cries day and night, Ah Yoong tells me. The girl doesn't complain, but who can say what she tells her parents?" Yee Mah puffed agitatedly.

"Even so, you treat her well!"

"True, Tai Ku, true! I, the mother-in-law, treat her well. I even let her sit in the shop with me. I introduce her to all my good customers. Meet my daughter-in-law, I say to them. I give her a lot of face, but our Ah Kiong doesn't want her in his room! What to do?"

"Is that so? Has he another woman outside?"

"How can a mother know such things?" Yee Mah was shaking her head. "He moves here and there, goes to the cabarets and bars! I even hired a detective! So much trouble and money he cost me! I couldn't write to tell you. Family shames must keep in the family; how to let the letter-writer know, right or not?"

Tai Ku nodded sagely, savouring every minute of this confidential exchange.

"Aiya, that son will kill me one day!" Yee Mah continued. "Last week he came home drunk, and then he pushed our Siew Lai out of his bedroom. Fat pig! Sow! He yelled at her. All kinds of names rolled out of his mouth. Water cannot clean off! You tell me, what will the in-laws say when they find out? And I still owe Siew Lai's father fifty thousand!"

"Is business no good then?" Tai Ku asked.

"Choy! Choy! Don't say that!" Yee Mah was superstitious, and where her shop was concerned, only auspicious things could be uttered aloud. "I want to do more business, to expand, and Siew Lai's father lent me the money. That son of mine, the things I do for him, ah, and he doesn't know! I ruin his life, he says. When I die, I'll leave him a good business. In our time, we did what we were told; no asking this and that and no complaining."

"Right, right!" Tai Ku agreed. "During our time, parents were the sky, children the earth! Now, ah, I'll be happy if no one accuses me of ruining Yoke-lin's life! Only last month, Tai Shook, he dared accuse me, said I rushed Yoke-lin into marriage!"

"Talking of our Yoke-lin, let me take her with me to the temple. Wash away her bad luck! Ask the medium to change her luck." Yee Mah glanced at Yoke-lin who had been listening all this while. "She can go back with me to Penang and work in the cabaret, mah! Not a young girl anymore. What harm? Now modern times. And more chances of meeting a rich man, right or not? Better than us last time. This small town here, which man, you tell me, which man wants a woman with a child? Right or not?"

6

The medium of a temple, much like a magician on stage, knows the power of visuals, form and ritual. He seeks to distract in order to sway his flock, emptying their minds but filling their hearts with hope, weakening their wills but strengthening their desires, exhorting their spirits to rise and their cash to flow. Constantly, he fans the flames of faith, desire and illusion. But this observation of a modern cynic, for better or for worse, had yet to touch the consciousness of the crowd gathered that morning at the temple of the Ninth Lord of the Heavens. The worshippers, mostly the wives of shopkeepers, traders and vegetable farmers, were milling in the temple compound, buying fresh flowers, baskets of fruits, bundles of joss papers, joss sticks and candles for the gods.

Large, green-tiled dragons arched over the temple roof while in the distance, on the eastern side of town, rose the white minaret of the mosque over a landscape of attap roofs and coconut trees.

The day was hot and the crowd noisy as the women jammed the entrances to the inner courtyard.

"Push to the centre, everyone! Push or be pushed aside!" Yee Mah shouted. "Come, follow me," she ordered and thrust her amah forward to lead the way.

Ah Yoong, taller and stronger than the rest of them, elbowed her way through the crowd with Yee Mah and Siew Lai in tow. Tai Ku and Yoke-lin, with little Yenti in her arms, followed.

"You can't speak to the gods direct," Yee Mah explained to her daughter-in-law. "That's why some people's prayers are not answered. In court, we need interpreters; in the temple, we need mediums. They know how to plead to the gods for us. They say this one is very good. The gods enter his body and do miracles. Mrs Khoo told me the other day about a very sad case. This woman from Klang got thrown out by the mother-in-law. Barren as a coconut shell, the mother-in-law scolded her. She came to the medium here, asked for a son and, this medium, very good man, helped her beget a son."

Her daughter-in-law turned a dull pink even as she nodded dutifully at this broad hint of why they were there.

"How can spirits enter us?" Yoke-lin asked.

"Aiya, very strange things can happen in this world so full of spirits. Remember the Cowherd and the Seven Sisters? Madam White Snake? Spirit of a snake marrying a man?"

Yee Mah handed the temple attendant a very generous donation which caused the man to bow low, thanking her again and again. He struck the drum three times to announce Yee Mah's donation to the gods. She was pleased and thought the act well worth the sum she had paid. That her business had prospered was proof enough of the power of these deities and the mediums who served them, and for Yee Mah, it was not so much the intensity of her belief as the winning of the spirits on to her side that really mattered. "Once the gods bless you, ah, everything you do will prosper!" she declared.

The sudden clashing of gongs sent all the devotees streaming into the temple hall where the life-size figure of the Ninth Lord of the Heavens fixed his porcelain gaze upon the women, jostling in the heat and incense smoke to get near him.

A sudden roll of drums and the women's chattering stopped. "All kneel!" the temple attendant bawled.

A resplendent figure in blue brocade swept into the hall, and the majestic incarnation of the Ninth Lord of the Heavens seated himself on the red and gilt throne. The women knelt and kowtowed as they would in the court of a Chinese mandarin. "Bring her in!" the attendant shouted again.

"Let me go, let me go! I'm not mad!" A screaming woman was dragged into the hall by two strong female attendants who forced her to kneel in front of the Immortal Lord. She hissed and clawed at her warders like a wild cat, the glitter of insanity in her eyes. "Yaaaaah! Mad-ah! Mad-ah!" she yelled at the top of her voice.

The Immortal Lord stood up and waved his red imperial seal over the unfortunate creature. "Demon of madness, I say to you let her go. I, the Ninth Lord of the Heavens, command you!"

The woman, screaming and rolling on the floor, dodged his seal this way and that as if it were some lethal weapon. The attendants grabbed her by the shoulders and pinned her down with the weight of their bodies, forcing her to kneel before the Lord. As he held his seal over her, chanting verse after verse in the familiar cadence of a Chinese prayer, the woman slumped forward, whimpering like a dog in pain, the glint of madness slowly fading from her eyes.

"Wah, strong power! The demon is gone. See, see her eyes!" the crowd murmured.

An old lady pushed her way through the crowd and kowtowed at the altar of the gods.

"Thank you, Master Loong, thank you! You have saved my daughter!" she cried. "She was so sad she wanted to kill herself and the children! Her husband, the brute, has no heart! He brought home another woman, a she-fox! Two women under one roof, how to have peace?"

The Lord shook his head. There was only so much that he could do, for in this weary world each must bear his own burden. Meanwhile, Tai Ku and Yee Mah were all the more determined that the medium should be asked to do something for Yoke-lin and Siew Lai. Yoke-lin was hoping too that some deity might point the way and set her on the right course of action to support herself and the baby. Her future was bleak, she knew, for few Chinese men would marry a woman and take another man's child into their family, and even if a man accepted her baby, his relations would call him a fool.

"Help me, Master Loong, give me a son, I beg you, give me a son. Six girls already! He'll leave me, he said, if the next one is another girl. Aiyoh, pity me, pity me and my daughters so young!" The large woman with the large breasts, hanging down like a sow's after too many litters, knocked her head several times on the hard stone floor.

Yenti wailed, kicking her little legs as she lay in Yoke-lin's arms. She hushed the protesting infant. The poor woman's plea, vibrating like an echo in the empty chambers of her heart, brought tears of sympathy and self-pity to her eyes.

Yee Mah coughed. Her heart had no room for such fine feelings which would lead to nothing. She was a practical woman and had already taken stock of her own situation and dynastic ambitions. A course of action which would ensure the continuity of the generations, her lineage, and the prosperity of her shop was already taking shape in her mind: a powerful medium to intervene with the gods, to give sons to a barren woman, to produce the coveted grandson for the cornerstone of her edifice, to induce Ah Kiong to go into Siew Lai's room, spend a few nights there, desire begetting life, wealth begetting more wealth, then all would be blessed and well with Prosperity Goldsmith.

The simplistic, the illogical and the irrational, merging with age-old tradition and desire, produced in Yee Mah's uneducated mind images unquestioned and unexamined, whose implicit logic and beauty were such that Yee Mah arranged for Siew Lai to have a private session with Master Loong.

"Aiya, Tai Ku, what would you have me do? Look at me; if not dyed, a head of white hair already! Look at Siew

Lai, young and sallow. We're women, we were young once, we understand the pain if the man doesn't come home. What has she to lose now? Two years already! Ah Kiong hasn't even been into her room once! I've only one son and one daughter-in-law! And the years pass in the blink of an eye!"

On their way home, an afternoon thunderstorm, sudden and short, broke over them. Strong winds bent the coconut trees and rain drops the size of fifty-cent coins splashed on to the car's windscreen.

"Good omen, Mistress Yee Mah, good sign! The heavens open! Water, a sign of wealth and fertility! Many many grandsons to come!" Ah Yoong exclaimed what her old mistress wanted most to hear, while her young mistress sat blushing beside her.

"Master Loong said it would rain!" exclaimed Tai Ku.

"Chieh! I just look at the dark clouds, I too can say it will rain!" Yoke-lin scoffed. She could not see how such a simple prediction of the weather could prove anything. "Just now he said my life would be difficult. I don't have to pay someone to tell me that!"

"Argue some more! What Master Loong said about your character is so true! Stubborn! Never listen to others! You will have trouble!" Tai Ku scolded her.

"Already in trouble," Yoke-lin murmured.

"Right, answer me back! That's the only thing you're good at! Earn more money? Ha! I daren't dream!" Tai Ku's screech was drowned by a sudden clap of thunder. "See, even the gods agree!"

"I will work," Yoke-lin said with quiet determination.

"Work? What work? Tell me, what work can you do here? Tap rubber? Is that enough to feed us? Your daughter doesn't grow, ah? Can live on one tin of milk a month, ah? Use your head! At my age, others are getting money from their children already. Me? I daren't even think of it!

Got to support daughter and granddaughter." Tai Ku stifled a sob and dabbed her eyes with the inevitable large white handkerchief.

"Aiya, Tai Ku, why cry? Chieh! Don't be so foolish. Yoke-lin here didn't say she won't come to Penang. Only said she doesn't believe in Master Loong. If she works in the cabaret in Penang, in no time, plenty of money for mother and daughter, right or not, Yoke-lin?" Yee Mah asked.

The wily aunt soothed and cajoled Tai Ku into good humour again, and Yoke-lin, mute with shame, could only nod and agree to all that the older women were planning for her.

"New shoes and five or six cheongsams," Yee Mah said. "Don't worry, I'll lend you the money first."

The car finally stopped outside the grocer's and the sun came out once more to shine upon the young mother and her baby girl.

"Come, ah, come upstairs for a cup of tea," Tai Ku, beaming once more, invited Yee Mah and her entourage.

Siew Lai, pouting her lips, shook her head, and Yee Mah, laughing indulgently, replied, "Too much trouble; another time, Tai Ku, another time. Our Siew Lai is tired. We go to the hotel."

"Nah, see with your own eyes how others look down on us," Tai Ku grumbled when the car door slammed shut, and that symbol of wealth rolled out of Ming Sun Lane. "Wake up! Don't sleep through life. Have money, have face, that's what people say!"

Yoke-lin followed her up the dark narrow stairs with the sinking feeling that somehow, her fate had been sealed once again.

Yenti's Journal

"You are of Hakka flesh but Cantonese bones!" said my grandmother, Tai Ku. "Every bone in you is Cantonese, because I brought you up." And so, brought up by my fiercely provincial and chauvinistic grandmother, I grew up secure about my roots, knowing that I belonged to that part of the Chinese community which the history books call "sinkehs".

Tai Ku regarded my Hakka forebears as beings lower than the Cantonese but I can understand her attitude. Her roots went back to the nineteenth century Taiping Wars between the Cantonese Ghee Hins and the Hakka Hai Sans in Perak's Kinta Valley.

In this valley, the immigrants had hewn and cut, mined and fought over mining rights, tin ore and women. A few became rich and the streets of Ipoh used to bear their names. But for every Chinese name that is known, there are nameless thousands like my grandfather, Tai Shook. For them life was two bowls of rice a day. And yet... they have hewn a niche for themselves in the Malay Peninsula, and produced graduate grandsons and granddaughters like me. It's something to be proud of, isn't it?

It's something to be proud of even though I don't know who my real father is or what my mother was like in her youth, except for pieces of gossip picked up from relatives. Mother doesn't talk about her past, that is, her real past. What she doesn't want to remember doesn't exist. If she knew that I am writing about her roots and origins, she would be furious. Fortunately, since she cannot read English, the problem will never arise.

And yet, why shouldn't one acknowledge one's roots? Reverse snobbery these days celebrates its humble pioneering origins, but the nouveau riche, like my mother in her grand mansion, dig out the successful family scholar or business tycoon to sing about. To listen to my mother these days boasting about her forebears, one would have thought that our family had come from men of vision and learning. The reality, in truth, is very different.

I have to write in order to understand. What I am writing may be fiction mixed with fantasy, but still, fiction is fantasy made real by a few facts.

Before writing, I had never associated my grandparents with the lower strata of Chinese immigrants who came in their nameless thousands, swarming into Singapore and the Malay Peninsula. Tai Shook was one of these, sold across the Nanyang for the price of a few dollars. I remember him as a silent man who gave me rides in a soap box, strapped to the back of his bicycle. As soon as I could walk, he took me everywhere on those days when he was not peddling pork. His pleasures were simple: eating durians by the roadside, breakfast at the corner coffeeshop, and drinking a soft-boiled egg out of a saucer. He too never spoke about his past. But he told me stories of ancient heroes which he had heard over the radio. I think, except for these stories, he had no past and no China.

I had never thought of him as an oppressed and ignorant immigrant forced to work in the tin mines. He was always Tai Shook, my grandpa-butcher in Ming Sun Lane, Ipoh. Did he miss me when Mother took me away to live with her in Penang? I don't even know when he died. Mother doesn't talk about him at all, except once, when she said that he had always lived under somebody's thumb. Was that her indictment upon his life? He had always accepted his fate. His favourite Cantonese phrase was, "Two bowls of rice to warm the belly". Was that all he wanted from life? Such an incredibly low and basic goal. But I have never known hunger.

When Tai Ku passed away, again Mother was silent.

She did not tell me, much less don black to mourn the passing of her adopted mother, and I was left to infer what I liked from her action. All she said was, "When I leave a place or a person, I pull up everything, roots and all."

Perhaps that was what happened to my father. All I know is that his real name is not Chow. "Why did you give me a fictitious name?" I asked my mother.

"You want the police to come after us? In those days, so dangerous. Your father ran into the jungle to join the Communists. I brought you up, gave you an education! He might as well be dead! And you question me?"

After that, she had refused to say any more. So my guess is that Mother and my grandparents must have suffered from the typical immigrant fear of the authorities, and chose to give me a fictitious father rather than face deportation back to China.

When I was twelve, Mother left Penang for Singapore, and I was farmed out to an Uncle Cheng in Alor Star, Kedah. He was the superintendent of Police in charge of rehabilitating ex-members of the Communist Party of Malaya. Three such men stayed in a lodge at the back of his house. Hardy middle-aged men, very skilful with their hands. One of them showed us how to skin a squirrel and pull a tortoise live out of its shell. He chopped it up and made a delicious tortoise soup for us. Poor man, he had surrendered himself because he was starving. He seemed more like an ignorant farmer lured by false ideals for which he paid with wasted years than a dangerous element out to subvert society. Sometimes I imagine that one of these had been my father and our meeting in Alor Star had been engineered by the gods.

My father was not the only man in the family to disappear after an unhappy marriage. Yee Mah's only son, Ah Kiong, played the disappearing game too. He disappeared after the birth of his son. Perhaps he reckoned that he had fulfilled his filial obligations to his mother. It was rumoured that the son could have come from the medium of the Ninth Lord of the Heavens. But who is to know the truth unless my aunt, Siew Lai, chooses to speak?

Anyway, every family has its skeleton in the cupboard. I used to be ashamed that Mother was a cabaret woman turned respectable housewife, and Grandmother Tai Ku was a prostitute turned matriarch. But now, seeing them as part of that wave of immigrants of Cantonese, Hokkien, Teochew, Hakka or Hock Chia origin, the impoverished and inarticulate (except for my grandmother) thousands who farmed and mined the land, who worked and married and produced descendants like me, assistant curator of a museum, I have chosen to give them a voice, and I am not ashamed of them any more.

Love

"That which gives me
A family, a home and a name
Is love."

An Orphan

7

Tawdry neon lights, a few drunken brawls, and one or two incidents involving wives in search of errant husbands had contributed to the rather seedy reputation of the Green Parrot in Penang. To the conservative nonyas of respectable Peranakan families on the island, the Green Parrot was a blight on the social and moral landscape. It was the duty of all virtuous women, they claimed - and that, of course, meant virtually all the first wives of the island's mercantile community and plantation owners - to keep their sons and husbands away from the cabaret.

But their men folk thought otherwise. For them, the Green Parrot was a haven of pleasure, a bright green spot on the arid plain of thrift and industry, an oasis where charming women laughed at their jokes and mopped their brows with hot scented towels.

Tonight, Mr Lam, the portly manager, was in earnest conference with a group of cabaret-mummies, the middle-aged women in charge of the younger dance hostesses. Penang's night life was once again blossoming, following the recent tin and rubber boom. A new cabaret had just opened down the road. Mr Lam was worried that the new competitor was luring away his patrons with more daring floor shows, and hostesses more liberal with their favours.

"You girls must look sharp!" he said.

"Hear that, girls?" Madam Tang turned to her charges, mostly young women from small towns and villages, lured by the urban bright lights.

Yoke-lin crossed her legs daintily, and adjusting the slits of her cheongsam, settled down to listen.

"Nah, listen, no wooden faces. Smile! You make them happy, they pay. Have a drink or two with them, help them forget wives and worries. Why they come here, you think? To forget, that's why! Don't act like spring chickens, like you don't know what men are like! If can't touch you here, can't touch you there, why you work here? A kiss here, a kiss there is nothing, just part of working, mah! Nothing to lose, plenty to gain, believe me! People have mouths. Word gets round, then wah, aiyoh-yoh, the men will line up for you. Then ah, hands stretched out, money comes. Easy! No bowl of rice is so easy like this to earn, right or not?"

Mr Lam nodded his approval. He knew he could depend on Madam Tang, and come the start of the Lunar New Year and a daring floor show, he would turn in a healthy profit. He'd show everyone that a former Chinese-educated clerk could be as successful as the English-educated. He simply had to be firm with the girls and not let them climb on his head, he reminded himself. They had been engaged to entertain patrons, so entertain them they must, unless they wanted the sack!

Times had changed, he told the dance hostesses. Guests used to be satisfied with a bit of female conversation and company. But not any more. Whatever arrangements the girls made with patrons after the cabaret had closed was none of his business; he wouldn't interfere.

When the new show opened, featuring the notorious Rose Chan, it was an instant hit, and attendances shot up to dizzying heights. Men from as far away as Bukit Mertajam came in droves. It was business by day and pleasure by night, enticed as they were by the sensuous dancer's gyrations with a python, in that crude portrayal of the story of the union between a Chinese scholar and the reincarnation of a white snake.

After each performance, scores of men booked the hostesses for dances and drinks, spending enough to keep Mr Lam happy for months. It was indeed a happy and prosperous New Year for him; he was promoted to managing director. A great personal triumph, and years later, he would recall this period fondly as the year in which he changed the island's taste and savoir-faire. He was proud of the few French and English phrases picked up from foreign patrons, who would have danced at the more prestigious E&O Hotel if not for him, Lam the Great Promoter.

"What about supper tonight, Yoke-lin?" he asked, sauntering up to the bar where she was drinking with Lily as usual. He eyed her glass of brandy with paternal disapproval. But the Yoke-lin tonight was no longer the Yoke-lin of a few years ago who had tottered into the Green Parrot on her first pair of stiletto heels.

"Wah, Mr Lam, invite Yoke-lin only, ah? What about old hens like us?" Lily wagged a crimson fingernail at him. "Yoke-lin, go on, ask him. He'll do whatever you ask!"

"So greedy, ah, Lily! Mr Lam, treat from you tonight?" Yoke-lin asked.

"My favourite girl opens her golden mouth, how can I say no?" Mr Lam sighed, tapping his heart, shaking his head and making a great show of being a fool in love.

"See! You ask only, okay! I ask, always no! Not a bad fish, this one. Better hook him!" Lily nudged her friend.

Yoke-lin shrugged and tried to look interested. But her eyes betrayed a vacuous look as she listened to the Cantonese singer crooning a love song to the crowd, swaying to the music, some in rhythm, body touching body, some awkward and stiff, stepping backwards and forwards, small town men out for the night and anxious to get their money's worth. She despised them as much as she despised herself.

Things had changed and moved in directions she had never foreseen. There had been little pleasure, or joy, or pain these five long years; nothing but a dull dutiful plodding, year by year, crawling forward like a prisoner counting the days towards his release, doing nothing important, gaining nothing in return. All that she had to show for these years was one little girl, a handful of bills and no savings.

Almost every cent she had earned had been handed over to Tai Ku for Yenti's upbringing. The girl's health was poor, Tai Ku said. Yenti needed herbs and medicine from China. There was not enough money to pay the doctor and the medium, another letter said. Then, Tai Ku herself became sickly with a persistent stomach ailment. Everything cost money and there was hardly enough.

Just before the Lunar New Year, she had returned to Ipoh, bearing gifts of new dresses, shoes, a doll and a toy pram for Yenti, packets of sweet meats for Tai Ku, cigarettes for Tai Shook and two new blouses for Ah Jen. Once again, however, she was disappointed that the visit, like all her other visits, had not been a happy one. Yenti was ill again. She was fretting in bed that day, her cheeks flushed with fever and her eyes bright with an undercurrent of energy. She became quite ill upon the slightest provocation, was quite spoilt and was in the habit of throwing tantrums.

When she had suggested, during that visit, that Yenti's diet be changed, Tai Ku had been quick to take offence.

"You think I don't feed your precious one enough food, ah?" she asked. "Everything she eats is steamed for hours! Fish roe, liver, pig's brain, frog's legs! Tell me, are these cheap?"

"No, Tai Ku, I know it's not cheap. But everything is steamed, and no fruits!"

"Wah! Now not happy with me, ah! All these years, you kept quiet! Not a word! And I the old fool work and work! Take her back with you then! Now not poor any more! Take her and look after her yourself!" Tai Ku had yelled.

At this Yenti had cried and clung to her grandmother.

"See, Tai Ku, Yenti wants you to look after her," she had tried to placate her mother.

"What for? Other people's daughter! You think I want to poison my own granddaughter? What do you know, you tell me? You see her everyday, ah? Once every few months! When she's sick, who looks after her? This old cow here, that's who! I know my place, only better than a servant! You think I take your money for myself?"

And so, they had quarrelled about money again. Money. Money. One way or another, it was always Yenti and money during each visit, and each time, she had forked out more money to cleanse her guilt and appease Tai Ku. The cubicle in Ming Sun Lane had begun to accumulate over the years, certain material comforts. A new wardrobe. A new set of table and chairs. A sewing machine for Tai Ku which was the envy of the tenants, particularly her good friend, Ah Por. There was even a Made-in-England bicycle for Ah Jen to ride to school. And yet, Tai Ku was always poor, always without cash for this and that, pawning off a gold ring or two and then showing her the pawn tickets. She had never failed to give her the money to redeem those ornaments. So what more did Tai Ku expect?

There was little comfort in her daughter. The child was extremely attached to Tai Ku and seemed to look upon her, the mother, as some kind of rich but distant aunt who brought expensive presents and who had to be kissed.

"Come, my precious, come and give your mama a kiss," Tai Ku had to coax the child; and Yenti would stand on tiptoe and gravely plant a kiss on Yoke-lin's cheek.

"Good girl, good," she had sighed; "go and play." She had not known what else to say to her little girl who was no longer a part of her. Yenti regarded her almost as a stranger, and although Yoke-lin was pained, she realised that a visit every three months or so wasn't good enough. The child hardly knew her. Sometimes she had wondered whether she had done the right thing to keep the girl. The father had disappeared without a trace. He was but a blur in her memory now. But the pain of being rejected had not ceased, only dulled. In idle moments, she had wondered sometimes whether what his people had said was true. Had he found her intolerably cold and ugly? She would never know.

Old Mrs Chow had later claimed that her son was a Chinese patriot, dedicated to his motherland. How very confusing. China was so far away. Sometimes, Yoke-lin wished she had stayed longer in school, like Ah Jen. Then, perhaps, her life might have been different. If only Tai Ku had not sent her out to work at twelve, she thought, and promised herself that she would send Yenti to school.

"Yoke-lin, ah, look over there. That Ah Kiong is here again with Ruby. What does he see in her? She looks old enough to be his aunty!" Lily sniggered.

"Kaypoh! He sees something you don't!" Yoke-lin replied a little impatiently, but she did not tell Lily that Ah Kiong was her cousin and Yee Mah's wayward son.

"Aiyoh! See how she clings to him! Like he will fly away or what?" the irrepressible Lily exclaimed again.

"You! Shhh! Ruby understands him. His marriage is unhappy. He was forced to marry his wife."

"I know. Ruby herself told me. The wife's fat," Lily giggled.

"Quiet! They're coming." Yoke-lin pinched her friend's arm.

"Yoke-lin, how? Eaten already?" Ah Kiong said.

He had never acknowledged Yoke-lin as his cousin and they had never discussed family matters. But although Ah Kiong knew that his mother had instructed Yoke-lin to keep an eye on him and to report on his activities, he had never held this against his cousin.

"Ah Kiong, so long already, you never give us a treat," Lily complained.

"Not tonight," Ruby answered for him. "Got trouble."

Ruby's thin face, caught in the momentary glare of a spotlight, looked dry and haggard despite her rouge.

"What's happened?" Yoke-lin asked.

"Bad luck, that's what," Ah Kiong replied gloomily.

"Tell them, Ah Kiong. No use hiding. Tomorrow, all the papers will be full of it," Ruby urged him.

But he kept quiet, unable to find the words to describe what had happened to Pearl, a young prostitute and a mutual acquaintance of the women.

"Bad luck, just bad luck!" Ruby shook her head. "Always come when you least expect it."

"Aiya, you two, talk this, talk that! What's happened?" Lily asked.

"Bad luck, that's what!" Ruby repeated. "Towkay Khoo - really choy, choy! - died in Pearl's room at the Khoo Kongsi! Pearl was with him, and then suddenly his heart stopped! Eyes wide open! The amah called the ambulance. They pulled him off the bed and quickly dressed him! Luckily, he wasn't stiff yet."

Ruby snorted like a horse trapped by its own fears, restless and rearing to go somewhere, anywhere, where the demons of life would not touch her.

"I quickly-quickly took Pearl to the temple to get rid of the bad luck. Don't know what evil this will bring! Such things are very unlucky, they say. And his eyes open, that is extra bad!" Ruby's hands were trembling as she lit a cigarette. "Like this, six or seven years bad luck! His spirit not at peace, right or not? Died so suddenly, and not in his own house some more! Like this, ah, they'll have to put his coffin in the garden."

"It's fate," Lily said. "That's our life, what to do? You dance only, you can't make ends meet. You want to earn more, then must do this and that. Trouble, always trouble. Ha! The day I hook a big fish, ah, I will quit!"

Lily's bitter face was thin and sallow, the result of smoking four to five packs a day. Five or six abortions and twice as many disappointments in love had left their scars on her. She was no longer the young girl who had left her village ten years ago.

Ah Kiong was puffing his cigarette in silence, letting the women talk. Yoke-lin could not tell whether he was feeling sorry for them.

"Bad luck strikes when you least expect it," he muttered. "Can't tell, but the Khoo family might give Pearl something to keep her quiet. They want face, not a scandal."

Ruby scoffed at Ah Kiong's optimism. "Ha! Who can tell? These rich people can do what they like. If Khoo's old wife wants revenge, then how? She might even send gangsters to beat up Pearl. Who's to tell? If I were Pearl, ah, I'd leave this town quickly!"

The previous year, a towkay's wife had gone to Ruby's lodgings with a truckload of broom-wielding female relations to ransack her room.

"Those witches smashed my dressing mirror! Years and years of bad luck now! The old witch cut up all my cheongsams. Not even one left! And that old Tan, where was he after all those promises? I never saw his face again! Hiding under his wife's sarong!"

"Aiya, forget it! Don't take it so badly," Lily advised. "In this world, if you can enjoy today, then better enjoy. Take what you can. If you get something out of them, good. If not, then your bad luck. A good man is usually afraid of his wife," Lily said sagaciously as she lit another cigarette.

"Not always! This one here is not afraid!" Ruby patted Ah Kiong's shoulders. He seemed embarrassed and edged away from her. "If good luck comes, this rich boy might want me. Concubine even, I don't mind." She laughed and tweaked his ear playfully. "Big towkay of goldsmith shop, mah! Once a month, must sleep with his wife. Once a month, his mother said, and then she even gives him money!"

Ruby and Lily laughed almost hysterically at the thought of it. Yoke-lin sipped her brandy and said nothing.

"Ah Kiong, when you become towkay, don't forget us! We'll go and pay our respects to your wife, the towkay-neo," Lily teased.

"What's so funny? I earn my money like you two," Ah Kiong replied sullenly. "Spend one night with her, I get money. An honest living, right or not?"

The bitter cynicism in his voice was unmistakable, and Yoke-lin winced a little at his hardness.

"If don't go to her, my desperate mother will send her sow somewhere else! All she wants is a little male pig!"

After Ah Kiong and Ruby had left, Yoke-lin and Lily waited for the cabaret to fill with men out to have a good time during the Lunar New Year holidays. Large, paunchy, balding Chinese traders with thick necks and sleek round faces, seated round the tables in the dim light.

"Like well-fed hogs," thought Yoke-lin. She suppressed a yawn. Night after night, with very little change, she had sat with such men.

"Ah, ah, what you want to drink?" one of them asked. He did not even bother to find out her name.

"Lime juice, thank you," she replied.

"What! Lime juice only? Cannot, cannot! You've got to drink with us tonight! Give her a brandy," the fat man beside her protested. "Ah Fook, brandy here!" he shouted to the waiter.

"Oi! Our towkay Kok Bun Tin very generous man," a trader in salted fish and eggs explained to her. "You do what he says and soon maybe you don't have to work here anymore!" he guffawed and patted her hand.

Later that night, a group of young men came in. They were all in their twenties, the scions of wealthy tin mining and trading families. Madam Tang greeted them eagerly.

"Jade, ah! Lily! Yoke-lin! Come, come, come! Welcome our young towkahs!" she shouted in her best Cantonese. "Master Kong, what wind blows you here tonight? I've not seen you for a very long time!"

"Not so free these days. I have to work for my living," Master Kong replied.

"Aiya! Our master here is so humble. Aaah, but they say the great are always humble." Madam Tang murmured the compliments reserved for honoured guests.

"No, no, Madam, not me! The great and rich is my cousin here, Lau Weng Chong from Weng Kong Goldsmith. He's your young towkay!" Master Kong laughed as he pushed forward a bespectacled young man.

"Aye, Master Lau, a happy and prosperous and evergreen new year to you!" Madam Tang rattled off, in rapid Cantonese, her stock of new year greetings, specially composed by the traditionalist to suit the young. "May you be alert as a dragon and vigorous as a stallion in the coming year!"

"Same to you, same to you," the shy young man murmured.

"Not the same, not the same!" Madam Tang laughed. "Too old, can't be too vigorous, mah!"

Master Kong whooped at this, and quickly came to his cousin's rescue. "Bring us your young and pretty girls then, Madam Tang! One young bird for each rooster! My friends," he turned to his group, "enjoy yourselves tonight. Big brother here will take care of everything! Waiter! Drinks for everyone!"

They sat down, each with an attractive hostess on either side of him, and raised their glasses to the Lunar New Year.

"Yaaaaaam Seng!" they shouted lustily in hearty Cantonese. "Once again, yaaaaam seng!"

Lau Weng Chong, young, intelligent and bespectacled like a typical Confucian scholar, put down his glass and turned to Yoke-lin.

"May I know your name?" he smiled.

"Pang Yoke-lin," she said.

"I'm Lau Weng Chong." There was a long awkward pause.

"You know how to dance?" she asked for want of something better to say.

Something in the eyes of the awkward young man beside her, made her want to put him at ease. She glanced at him again. Their eyes met, and a shy smile flashed across his boyish face.

"My first visit here," he grinned. "I don't know how to dance very well." His boyish charm was infectious, and she felt light-hearted and ready for a dance. She had liked him at once, despite the old-fashioned horn-rimmed glasses perched on his nose. His gentle voice and unassuming ways matched his pale delicate face. Such a contrast to his boisterous cousin.

"Master Kong can dance very well," she said.

"What's that? I heard my great name mentioned!" the cousin shouted from across the table.

"I said what a good dancer you are!" Yoke-lin shouted above the din of the band and the throng. The cabaret was packed with New Year revellers, waiting to see a special performance by the Infamous Rose.

"Thank you, thank you," Master Kong stood up and bowed so absurdly that everyone laughed. "Come, come, no sitting down! Dance everybody, dance! One two three, go!"

The whole group of grinning young men and giggling hostesses followed him to the dance floor so packed with swaying waltzing bodies that there was hardly any space left to move. Lau Weng Chong led Yoke-lin to the edge of the crowd, avoiding the crush of bodies in the centre, and holding her at a gentlemanly distance, not pressing against her like most other men, he glided slowly with her round the dance floor till they were back at their table again.

"You dance very well, Mr Lau," she said .

"Miss Pang, just call me Weng Chong. I'm not a big shot like my cousin."

"Then call me Yoke-lin. I, too, am not a big shot!"

They laughed gaily, the ice broken.

"Come and sit down and talk with me. You're different. Why are you a dance hostess?" he asked.

Yoke-lin felt awkward but pleased. To be told that she was different from Lily and the others was high praise to her. In her heart, she had never perceived herself as one of them.

"It's a very long story," she murmured.

"I'm so sorry. Please accept my apologies, I didn't mean to be inquisitive, or to embarrass you," he said, bowing his head.

"No, no, it's really all right."

"Look, er ... I mean, er ... can we go outside for a while? It's so noisy here."

"You're the patron," she replied softly. "We try to please you. Ask Madam Tang."

The cabaret-mummy was only too pleased that Mr Lau had found a girl he liked, and soon the two of them were walking into the cool dark night.

"Shall we go to the esplanade?" he asked. "It's very quiet there."

"Anywhere you like," she murmured, and was a little surprised at her own sudden shyness.

"First time I'm celebrating new year like this," he confided. "But since I'm going to England, my cousin says I must learn to dance."

"You can speak English?" she asked.

"Only a little. But I have to learn English to study in England.

"You rich people are so lucky," she sighed.

"Fated," he said.

"You really think so? Born into a rich family, you

end up somewhere high up; born into a poor family, you end up nowhere. Is it fate or wealth?" She waited for his reply.

"I know our society is unfair," he said after a long pause. "It's difficult. We rich become richer, you poor become poorer. That's why Mao Tse-tung wanted to change China."

"But that's communist!" she exclaimed, recalling the fears of the villagers.

"In my high school, we read his works, and I know he wants to make society more equal."

The earnest scholar spoke enthusiastically of Mao's vision, impressing upon the cabaret girl that in Mao's scheme of things, her lowly status would be exalted, and young men and women like them should fight for the glory of their Chinese homeland, the land of their forefathers. A strong sea breeze blew a fine salt spray into their eyes as they strolled up and down the almost deserted esplanade.

Finally weary, they sat down upon a stone bench and watched the advancing and retreating waves, listened to the rhythmic splashes, and talked of this and that, of ordinary hopes and fears shared by young men and women everywhere.

For a while, Yoke-lin forgot herself, with the taint of a failed marriage behind her and the responsibilities of motherhood before her. The young man with the deep and earnest voice was telling her about the changes in the world, and actually seeking her opinions as if she were as highly educated as him. A heady feeling of camaraderie bound them as she listened to him.

"Attitudes are changing. Men and women work as equals, shoulder to shoulder, to tame the earth for the good of our nation. No nation, no home," he quoted from his books.

"What about women like Rose Chan and me?" she asked.

"You and women like you, all exploited. Exploited by the capitalists and imperialists! You think Mr Lam the manager cares about you sincerely? What his bosses think, that's important!"

His sentiments were typical of those idealistic Chinese students of the fifties, products of private Chinese schools who looked to China and not the Malay Peninsula as the land of their hearts. Born and bred in a ghetto, mainly a ghetto of the mind, the cabaret girl could only point out, "But you're from a rich family!"

"Don't mix me with others," he cautioned her. "My great grandfather was a landless peasant, and poor, very poor," he defended his background quickly. "Ourfamily suffered great hardship. Then they found tin on the land my grandfather bought. Our family fortune is based on tin."

"You like China so much, why then do you want to go to England?" she asked.

"Duty, duty," he sighed. "It's my mother. My uncle advised her to send me there to study engineering, so that I can come back and take charge of the tin mines. That's what my mother and uncle want, not what I want!" He sounded almost petulant, like a spoilt child.

8

The Lunar New Year was coming to an end. On the seventh day, the Cantonese celebrated Mankind Day with the traditional raw fish salad which they tossed with chopsticks for good fortune in the coming year. On the ninth day, the Hokkiens celebrated thanksgiving and prayed to the God of the Sky, burning the tops of the sugar cane plants to commemorate an event, hundreds of years ago, when the Hokkiens hid in the sugar cane plantations after their defeat by the Cantonese in a savage provincial war in China. The Cantonese had promptly set fire to the sugar cane plantations. A fire which had raged for three days and three nights. Thousands of Hokkiens had died. The people in desperation prayed to the God of the Sky for rain. He took pity on them and sent a storm to put out the fire. From that day onwards, according to Yoke-lin's landlady, a Hokkien herself, the Hokkiens had always celebrated the New Year with sugar cane.

On the last day of the New Year, Yoke-lin went to the goldsmith shop in Temple Street to pay her respects to Yee Mah. Temple Street that morning was a river of red paper, the residue of the strings of fire crackers lit by the shopkeepers to usher in the God of Wealth upon opening their shops for business once again.

The morning sun, bright as a newly-minted coin, shone in a clear blue sky so that if one were to look towards the hills, one could almost see the tiny cable train climbing up Penang Hill.

Prosperity Goldsmith and Company had a carpet of red fire cracker papers lining its shop front. All the lights in the shop were blazing, and gold chains, bracelets and bangles glittered in their glass cases.

"Good luck and prosperity in the new year, Miss Yoke-lin," the shop assistant greeted her.

"Thank you and same to you, Tai Fook," Yoke-lin replied.

"Go in quickly. Our Siew Lai gave birth to a boy last night. A son-lor! Our old mistress is very happy, can't eat, can't sleep, smiling all the time." Tai Fook grinned.

Yoke-lin hurried inside to offer her congratulations. The long-awaited grandson had arrived at last! The family altar was ablaze with lights as bright as the shop front. Bronze lamps shaped like lotuses were lit beneath the portraits of the Eight Immortals, the Goddess of Mercy and Yee Mah's husband. Her old man's benign face gazed vacantly out of its old frame, and Yee Mah, with joss sticks in her hands, was bowing before it.

"Yee Mah, good luck and good health! Tai Fook just told me. You must be very very happy!" Yoke-lin said.

"Sit down, sit down. The old man's eyes have opened at last." Yee Mah tilted her chin towards her husband's photograph. "Last night after dinner, Siew Lai complained of pains. Not so soon, we thought; not due till next week, the doctor said. Lucky I made the driver stay back. One hour later, Siew Lai was still crying. Aiya, like this cannot, I said to her. Go, go to the hospital quick! If we had waited, she would have given birth in the car!" Yee Mah was eager enough to talk about the birth.

"How is Siew Lai?" Yoke-lin asked.

"Mother and son are very well, coming home soon. I don't like hospitals, especially going there during the new year."

"But born in the year of the horse, very good for a boy, Yee Mah," Yoke-lin said, knowing well this was what the old lady would like to hear.

"Hear that, Ah Loh Yeah (Old Man)? I hope you're satisfied," she turned to address her husband's photograph. "I've kept my promise. Your family now has a grandson!

Bless and guard him well. Make sure, ah, he's not like your own son!" Yee Mah was speaking loudly as though to someone quite deaf. "Aiya, Yoke-lin," she turned around once again, "I dress well and eat well, but who knows what troubles I have in my heart? Ah Kiong, I haven't seen him many days now. Do you know where he is?"

Yoke-lin shook her head, refusing to be drawn into spying for her aunt.

"You're useless! I thought getting you into the Green Parrot, you can tell me things about Ah Kiong! But never mind now. The gods protect those who pray to them. Siew Lai is, luckily, a good daughter-in-law. Every month, without fail, ah, she goes to the temple, stays three or four days, meditate and fast. Master Leong is very good to her. Each time, very strange you know, Siew Lai returns from the temple, Ah Kiong also comes back. Don't say you don't believe. It's true. Ah Kiong always comes home for money when Siew Lai comes back. Then I make him go to her. I scold him, I don't spare him. A man's heart is like a needle in the ocean bed. It pricks you where it most hurts, right or not? I scold my old man too." She pointed to the photograph again. "*Your* son, I say. Do something! But now that I've got the grandson, I'll stop."

"Right, Yee Mah, don't tire yourself," Yoke-lin said politely.

"You're young still. And don't say your Yee Mah always nag. I only want your good, mah. Another year has gone by-lor. Still single. When are you going to stop and settle down, ah?"

"Not easy to find a good man, Yee Mah, especially in the Green Parrot," Yoke-lin muttered.

"What about Mr Lam? I hear he's after you."

"Aiya, Yee Mah, he's got a wife and children, and he's old enough to be my father!"

"Yoke-lin, now don't say I talk too much. Just advising you, ah, and only because Tai Ku wrote to me. Your adopted mother is worried-lor! Twenty-four going on twenty-five, not young for a woman like you. Married before, and with one daughter, you can't marry a younger man. Which man, you tell me - and don't say Yee Mah here insults you, I'm just being frank - which man wants second-hand goods? And another man's child? Think again, I advise you, ah. If Mr Lam wants you to be his mistress, count yourself lucky. You're not growing any younger. What about Yenti, even if you don't think for yourself? What about Tai Ku? She's growing old-lor!"

When Yoke-lin still remained silent, Yee Mah continued.

"I can see you're clever, Yoke-lin. Not like the others. You think, ah, think a bit more. You think you can work in the cabaret forever? Every woman in the Green Parrot, ah, wants a home too. But you think Mr Lam will offer them one? He too has eyes, mah, and only those who can rise above the pack, as they say, will get out of there, and not suffer poverty. Every woman needs a home of her own, ah, especially those of us who have moved around."

Moving around was Yee Mah's euphemism for those days when, together with Tai Ku, she travelled from town to town, selling her services to the tin miners. And today, contented in her own good fortune, she was repeating again her theme of the women who sacrificed their virtue to save their families from starvation in China. That was no shame, she said, that was the duty of daughters. Even the Hongkong films showed this nowadays, she said. But having looked after their families, they must also look after themselves, marry a man who can provide a roof over their heads and three bowls of rice a day.

Yee Mah was realistic and hard-headed, a shrewd woman of business, and according to her, older men like Mr Lam, searching for an affirmation of their attraction still for women, would be willing to settle for less, having less of themselves to offer other than money. If she, Yee

Mah, had been as choosy as Yoke-lin, why, she would never have become the proprietress of Prosperity Goldsmith now. Rise with every step that you take, she said, for that was how people prospered - not by clinging to virtue, and certainly not by being choosy.

Yee Mah settled into her armchair and counted her prayer beads with the air of one who knew that she had done extremely well for herself. The interview was over. Yoke-lin rose to take her leave, but not before promising to give the subject of Mr Lam some thought, and to return for the baby's First Moon.

9

The sign said, "Weng Kong" (Ever Bright) Goldsmith in large red Chinese characters. Behind the shop counter sat the proprietress's son, Weng Chong (Ever Loyal). The young heir was flicking through the Chinese daily, the mouthpiece of his community on the island.

He was a little confused. There was talk of Malay independence and the stake for the Chinese in such a situation. There were letters about returning to one's homeland, on the one hand, and on the other, letters about going west to learn as much as one could from the foreigners, to equip oneself with the sort of skills which would make one indispensable to a fledgling nation. His mother and eldest uncle favoured the latter course, and wanted him to learn something of the family's business before he left for England. He was obeying them now, but he found the retail end of the business dull and boring. Often there was nothing to do except read the papers or gaze at passers-by.

The hot dry spell had arrived with the Lunar New Year and the long dreary days of stifling heat and humid air had begun. A thick blanket of tropical heat lay over the town wilting under an azure sky which blazed so blue that it hurt the naked eye. At such times, Weng Chong, bored with the ennui of a shopkeeper waiting for the customer, dreamed of running away from home to do great things, to dedicate his life to an all-consuming cause. If only he was not the only son! If only his mother was not a widow and devoted mother! His mother had slaved all her life for him, and him alone, and whatever he might feel in his heart, he would never want to cause her pain.

"A man can have as many wives as he likes, but only one mother," his uncle used to say, and from a young age,

Weng Chong had been taught to respect his mother highly because, although she had been widowed at a very young age, she had remained in the Lau family and devoted herself to bringing up Weng Chong as the heir to his father's estate. The popular Cantonese opera, "Sam Leong Taught Her Son", celebrates this maternal devotion in young widows who brought up sons to pass the imperial examinations and become scholar-magistrates in the old days in China. Weng Chong, too, undoubtedly hoped that one day he would pass the modern equivalent of the ancient imperial examination and bring honour to his mother and family.

Such a noble goal, however, seemed a little out of place on such a very hot day. Indian labourers mopped their brows in the shadow of the shophouses, crouched by the drain, drinking hot coffee out of discarded tin cans, their backs gleaming with the sweat of labour. Just across the road from Weng Chong and yet so far away from his world of Chinese wealth and Chinese hopes, an old wizened Indian sent a jet of betel nut juice out of the corner of his mouth. The red stream plopped into the drain, and the old man wiped his stained mouth on a corner of his dhoti. Weng Chong turned away and went back to reading his newspaper.

Thus vacantly occupied, he was surprised when on looking up, he saw Yoke-lin walking past his shop.

"Hullo, Miss Pang!" he hailed.

"Mr Lau! You work here?" She was just as surprised to see him behind the shop counter.

"Yes, er, no, just helping my uncle," he stammered. "Please, please call me Weng Chong. And, er, and I'll see you tonight."

Yoke-lin nodded, conscious of the curious stares of the other shop assistants. She hailed a trishaw hurriedly and told the rider to go to Trengganu Lane, anywhere, to get away from the young man who had intruded into her life.

The trishaw rider pedalled furiously, swearing in loud crude Hokkien at a bus which had lumbered by too closely. He swerved, almost throwing Yoke-lin out of her seat. The bus stopped just in front of the cooked food shop, sputtering to a halt and spraying yet another film of dust on to the trays of fried fish, boiled cuttlefish, stir-fried vegetables, soya bean cakes, fish balls soaked in chillie sauce, pork broiled in dark soya sauce, and pork liver and innards steaming in a thick oily sauce.

This was Chinese hawker food at its dirtiest, and according to some gourmets, at its tastiest. No one, including Yoke-lin who had stopped by the shop to purchase its wares, minded that the hawkers' aprons, once white pieces of cloth cut from flour sacks, were now stained a dirty brown. No one minded that the same pair of oily hands slicing a piece of pork fat a minute ago, was now counting out filthy dollar notes for a customer, and after that, would return to slice yet another piece of pork. Grease smeared the glass panes of the counter, the bowls and chopsticks; the chairs and tables were covered with a film of lard and lard oozed from the faces of the workers and customers guzzling their porridge. Pork fat and grime, the mark of the China man, lined the walls and floor of the shop.

Yoke-lin bought a packet of the pork cooked in soya sauce, and walked down Soochow Lane. A row of two-storey townhouses lined each side. Built at the turn of the century and reminiscent of ugly Victorian townhouses, they were decorated with ornate curves, arches and gaudy mosaic tiles. This once glorious row of mercantile wealth had faded with the years, and poorer families had moved in. One of the houses was a gambling den, and the house next to it, the residence of prostitutes with cubicles for hire by the hour. It was rumoured that a housewife, having lost all her housekeeping allowance at the mahjong table, could recoup her loss by slipping into that house of disrepute for an hour or two, and her husband would be none the wiser.

Lily, who lived down the lane, was not averse to earning some extra money in this manner. Why! Everybody was doing it, and she would be a fool not to.

"No smoking, no drinking, no gambling, what are you living for?" she asked Yoke-lin.

"Love and family," Yoke-lin answered, but not without a trace of doubt in her voice. Lily seemed to know so much more about life than she did.

"Love! Ha! Can it fill you when you're hungry?"

Before Yoke-lin could reply, the door of Lily's bedroom creaked open, and a pale-looking girl came in.

"Sister Lily?"

"Pearl, what is it?" Lily asked.

"I ... I've come to say good-bye."

The girl stood with head bowed after her speech as if waiting for Lily to dismiss her. She was a fair girl with delicate features and could not be more than sixteen.

"Aiya! Why you leave so soon?" Lily asked.

"Ah Lan Chay said we have to go. Thank you for everything, Sister Lily."

Someone shouted her name from the hallway and the girl left the room immediately.

"That one Pearl, ah? So young," Yoke-lin said.

"What so young! Twenty already!" Lily snorted.

"But she doesn't look twenty."

"She's always inside the house, only go out at night, mah. Ah Lan Chay follows her everywhere! Every cent that girl earns goes to her mother. She supports her whole family. All her brothers and sisters go to school. Ah Lan Chay says she's filial. Ha! I say she's stupid! Her mother cries only, and Pearl will work harder. Five, six men a night! Ah Lan Chay gets them for her. This time Ah Lan Chay has broken her rice bowl."

"You can't blame her. How could she know the old man would die in Pearl's room like that?" protested Yoke-lin.

"Ha! Another innocent one!" Lily scoffed. "That's what Ah Lan Chay wants! Aiya, so stupid! Then she can squeeze money out of the old stick's family, mah! You think they want a scandal? If people know that the old towkay died in Pearl's room, where can the family hide their faces?"

"How much is the family giving them?"

"Ha! Not a cent! That's why I said Ah Lan Chay had broken her rice bowl, mah. The old man's brother also got cheated last time. He wants to report to the police! Think of it, ha! Ah Lan Chay and Pearl will run like crabs have pinched them!" Lily laughed.

"But Pearl is so sweet. How can she ...?" Yoke-lin began.

"Aiya, what do you know? She started young, very young. This is the only life she knows. Ah Lan Chay asks her to sit, she sits, to stand, she stands. Like she's under her spell."

"Aiya, Lily, where got such powerful magic in this world?"

"Don't say you don't believe! Got money, you can find the medium. Money can make even the devil work!" Lily snorted. "Got good mediums and bad mediums. Some are tricksters and gangsters, but some can be good men."

Lily's faith in them was not unlike Tai Ku's and Yee Mah's. There were spirits floating in this world and their services could be bought and harnessed for one's good; the trick was to find the right medium.

"I really must find one to change my luck," Lily continued. "Lost again last night."

"Lily, you never learn! How can you save anything? Every cent goes to mahjong." Yoke-lin nagged, even though she knew it was futile.

"What to do? Can't seem to stop!" Lily laughed a gritty little laugh, the corners of her mouth curling in a sneer at her own weakness. "The spirits pull me there each night! I can't chop off my right hand again. Done it already, mah!"

Once, Lily had lived comfortably as the respected concubine of a rich trader, and she would have remained quite well off if the trader had not thrown up his hands over her gambling debts which he had to settle for her time and time again. Eventually, he had refused to give her any more money unless she swore to give up gambling. Lily cried and begged but the trader was adamant. Lily was desperate. Gambling was her drug but no one was willing to lend her any money. So when the trader finally came a-calling again, Lily rushed into the kitchen, grabbed a chopper, and kneeling on the floor, called upon Heaven and Earth to be her witnesses - she would chop off her right hand if she ever stepped into a gambling den again! It was a most melodramatic scene. People gathered round and the rich trader was magnanimous in front of an audience. He took out his wallet and handed Lily five hundred dollars. In less than a week, however, Lily was back in the gambling den. "Incorrigible!" the towkay bawled. But he continued to visit her and gave her small sums of money even though Lily was no longer his concubine.

"What hold have you over him? Black magic?"

Lily laughed. "If there's one thing I know how to do, it's to please a man! I give him his money's worth." She hooted as she patted her large soft breasts and lit a cigarette. She was Yoke-lin's only friend at the cabaret, and whatever her faults, Yoke-lin valued her friendship.

"You're still young; not like me, over the hills-lor!" Lily said, her tone more serious now. "Think about yourself. Tai Ku's sure to want you to be Lam's mistress; he's got money, mah. But will you be happy? In this life, ah, if you don't máke yourself happy, who will?"

10

When Weng Chong came at the appointed hour, they went to the beach again. The great sweeping shore of sand with the long breakers that plunged and ran in a hiss of foam was an oasis of emptiness. Except for one or two couples huddled against the stone embankment, there were only the two of them, facing the dark expanse of sea and sand in the gathering darkness.

It was a warm evening and the night insects were out. Yoke-lin swept away an ant, dizzy with the on-rush of ambivalent feelings as she listened to him enthusing about books, authors, theories about nation-building, the motherland, school and friendship. Inflamed by his own oratory and sliding from one emotion to another, he had not spoken like this with anyone before, he said.

"Do you think I read too much? Think too much?"

"A man should do what he thinks is best," she answered, and he was happy.

"I want to study again," he said. "One year in the shop is too long, I feel like a prisoner. I, er, I want to write poetry. But my family doesn't understand. My father was a government clerk. But his English was not very good. Unless we improve ourselves, you know, we Chinese will always be under the British. That's why I want to go to England, learn from them. Then my uncle wants me to go into our family business, like my cousin. Mother agrees, and, aiya," he sighed a little, "you know what mothers are."

Here they were on common ground and spoke at great length on the iron hold mothers have over their children.

"The maternal spirit never dies in a woman," he recited. "The root of heaven and earth, it binds, forever, the woman to the fruit of her womb."

"That's so beautiful," she said.

"I wrote it," he replied modestly.

"You write well," and she was full of admiration for him. "I wish I were as highly educated as you."

She got up from the stone bench where they had been resting. He followed her and side by side, they strolled towards the main road.

"I've always wanted to meet someone who can understand me," he began, "and you - you're not like those other low women. Why do you work there?"

She continued walking beside him, avoiding his eyes, her hands pressing down the skirt which the sea breeze was trying to raise. He did not speak again but gazed mutely at the young woman who was struggling to hold back her tears. He had yet to discover how to console and comfort a woman for he was only twenty-one and this was the first time that he had ever come this close to one of them other than his own beloved mother. How his untried heart ached for the girl beside him. He did not know that what he wanted, most of all, was to hold her close to his chest and ease the ache in there.

"It's my fate," she blurted. "I was an orphan. At eight, and, and ..."

She poured out her sad tale of the orphan of a battered mother, laying out her whole history before him, all except the one little fact that she had a daughter. Weng Chong held her hand, humbled by her suffering.

"My own life is so cushioned, so protected," he murmured, conscious of her nearness and the fragrance of her hair. Life had been hard on her, he thought, but she had retained something soft and sincere. He noticed how her breasts swelled inside her blouse as she was talking, how fair was her neck, and how smooth were those shoulders under the thin muslin. He took her hand and walking on in silence, entwined his fingers with hers.

She did not resist as he circled her waist with a timid arm, for here was a friend at last, an artist and scholar who appreciated her as his equal. And who could tell? He might be the gateway to a new life too. She was enchanted as she caught a new view of his features, the street lamp bringing out the seriousness in his eyes, the shadows in his cheekbones and the depression in his temples. He seemed like an upright man of strength.

"You regret already what you told me?" he whispered, a mischievous gleam in his eyes.

"So quiet here," she said "All the people gone."

"I'll walk you home then," and at her lodgings, they parted that night, neither coy nor uneasy. But like those who have peeped into each other's heart, they understood without the need for words.

The rains came in March, bringing grey skies and strong winds. Yoke-lin listened to the swallows' cries under the eaves of the shophouses, the gushing of the rain water down the drains, the slosh of mud in the streets and the tick-tock, tick-tock of the noodle hawker at midnight. That which was dead in her was slowly coming to life again, like young lallang shoots after the rains.

If Yoke-lin had questioned whether this was all an illusion, temporary and fleeting, she did not pursue the question long enough to get an answer, preferring instead to listen to the hiss of the dancing foam along the esplanade. Each night she was at the Green Parrot, her place of work, where she laughed and joked with the patrons, entertaining them with snatches of Cantonese love songs. But all the time she felt that her real life awaited her outside the Green Parrot. She was light of heart and smilingly refused Mr Lam's innumerable invitations to supper after the cabaret had closed.

Weng Chong came for her every night. Rain or shine, he waited to walk her home. Sometimes he was moody and silent, his face a thunder cloud, fighting off the anger just thinking of her dancing with the other men and he could do nothing about it. Sometimes he was eloquent and starry-eyed, waxing poetic under the cool moon, dreaming the dreams of a young man eager to claim his place in the world. But always, whatever his mood, he would wait for her at the cabaret entrance, ready to lay claim on her, and it pleased her that he was jealous of the hours she spent inside.

"But I've got to work. My family needs the money," she explained.

"I know."

That was all he could say, his young shoulders stiff with wounded pride. But whenever it rained, he would hold a large waxed-paper umbrella over her, and was cheerful and gentle as she clung to him, feeling his warmth under the damp clothes. He held her firmly in one arm and guided her expertly across drains and puddles, laughing at her helplessness as she tottered beside him on her high heels. At such times, they were like two young travellers finding their way home, and he appeared the more seasoned of the two.

At night, the rain trees in Central Park stood like dark majestic umbrellas in the dewy moonlight. The lawns were soaked but they had nowhere to go and so, huddled under the same umbrella, they strolled up and down the muddy paths.

"You're the most important thing that has happened to me," Weng Chong was speaking earnestly. "I know I've got to study. Please, wait for me. If you're patient, we, er, we ..."

"Weng, you're dreaming," she stopped him before he could continue. Her reply did not betray how much her heart had wanted to believe in his dream.

"I've got to go to England; everything's planned. My mother has dreamed and planned for me since my birth. I can't disappoint her," he said.

"I know. Besides, your mother would never accept me," she pointed.

"I will tell her how good you are, how unlike the rest. Mother's a kind woman. I've never heard her speak badly about anyone. She'll accept you once she gets to know you. I'm sure of it. If she knows how virtuous you are ..."

"Weng, stop," she said. "I'll never be virtuous in her eyes."

"You are mine," he replied, grasping her hand tightly. "Listen, wait for me. Keep ourselves busy, and the years will fly. Three years. I'll write everyday."

He was so earnest that she had not the heart to tell him her misgivings that night. Why spoil his happiness when it would be short-lived anyway? If fate would have it, a new life would open out for her, and she had no intention of deceiving him for long. She would wait. Not now. Not when they were so close, like any other young couple. That bit about her daughter could wait; just a bit more time to feel young and unburdened, she comforted herself as she rested her head on his thin shoulders. His face was pale and tired.

"You're not getting enough sleep." She smoothed away his frown. "Don't come tomorrow night. Too many late nights not good for you."

"You don't know what you're saying!" He shook his head. "All day I wait for night. I think of nothing but you. I wait for mother to go to bed. Most nights, I just walk the streets till it's time to come and fetch you."

"Poor scholar you, I don't want you to waste time. You should be reading, right?"

But all the same, she was pleased and patted his hand affectionately.

"It's better if I'm not at home," he continued. "Twice

tonight mother asked me what was wrong. She was worried."

"What did you tell her?" she asked anxiously.

"What could I say?" He laughed a little. "That my life is empty without you?"

She could see that he was angry with himself for failing to tell his mother about them. He was holding her tightly but very chastely. He refused to kiss her, and he had never done so. He did not want to cheapen their relationship, he explained, for he would never be like the other men, taking advantage of a woman in her position. He wanted to keep things pure and unsullied. She could sell her companionship like a geisha, but not her body. He wanted a virtuous wife as a virtuous daughter-in-law for his mother, and if they had done nothing shameful, that would make her more worthy in his mother's eyes. His own mother, he told her proudly, had never re-married, remaining faithful to the memory of only one man, his father.

He was proud of his mother and proud of his own broad-mindedness. He was not one to look down upon those whom circumstances had pushed into unworthy work. And as he traced the sandy paths with the woman he loved, he was not fully conscious of a deep-seated desire to liken himself, however tenuously, to the scholar-hero of old who had befriended and married intelligent courtesans, fighting off social prejudice and injustice, and finally, emerging righteous and triumphant, having passed the imperial examination and returned as a magistrate to his home-town to rescue his beloved from the clutches of a narrow-minded citizenry.

Yoke-lin too dreamed her own sweet dreams that night. To be admitted to the ranks of wealth and respectability, to acquire an honest family name and plant herself upon such fertile ground, was the length and breadth of her vision. So, even if Weng Chong did seem a little young and immature at times, she was not averse to being his wife if that was what fate had in store for her. It was a hundred times better than being Mr Lam's mistress, she thought, and she was not about to dissuade him from trying to convince his mother that she would be a worthy wife for him.

11

Pink table cloths covered the twenty tables laid with gleaming china bowls and chopsticks for the more than a hundred guests gathered at Prosperity Goldsmith. The tables were crammed into the shop front, between the pillars of the verandah, and spread out on to the five-foot way along Temple Street. Relatives, friends and business associates were standing up, table by table, and crying "Yaaam Seng!" to the matriarch of Prosperity Goldsmith.

"Thank you, thank you. So very kind of all of you!" Yee Mah beamed till her eyes were mere slits in her happy face.

Tai Ku, her younger daughter, Ah Jen, and five-year old Yenti were not the only ones who had travelled from afar to be present at this momentous occasion, to bring gifts and offer their congratulations to the matriarch. Yee Mah's neighbours, the proprietors and traders along Temple Street, the doctor who had delivered the baby, the monks and abbots of the temples, and the now famous medium of the Ninth Lord of the Heavens, all clapped and cheered when short and tubby Siew Lai waddled in carrying the precious month-old grandson and heir to Prosperity Goldsmith.

The baby boy was wrapped in a pink blanket, his tiny wizened head almost hidden by a pink woollen cap. He was decked out with gold chains round his neck, bracelets and anklets. And someone had pinned a large red amulet on his vest to ward off evil spirits.

"Such a high forehead, good sign for a boy! He'll reach high and do well," an uncle declared.

"Yee Mah, he's got your nose, ah, can smell out business!" the balding proprietor of the furniture shop next door teased her.

This was clearly Yee Mah's hour of triumph; it was as if she had produced the boy herself and secured the continuity of the Chan family.

"Where's Ah Kiong?" his father-in-law asked.

"Our Master Kiong will come downstairs soon," Ah Yoong quickly replied lest it be said that the son of Prosperity Goldsmith was indifferent not only to his wife but also to his newborn son.

Most relatives would consider a man's distance from his wife a private matter but they would not be so tolerant if the man did not even appear at the feast celebrating his first-born son. That would be a gross insult to his in-laws, and a show of indifference to the feelings of his relations and ancestors whose blessing the family should seek if it hoped to prosper.

"Tell Ah Kiong, he must come down. Tell him I will let him have what he wants," Yee Mah whispered to the amah.

"Aiya, I'll go and call him again." Ah Yoong slipped away from the feast.

"Come, come, everyone! Don't wait for me to come round to every table to serve you. Please help yourselves!"

Yee Mah raised her pair of chopsticks and plunged it into the dish of steamed chicken; her guests followed suit. One dish after another was brought in. After the steamed chicken, the plates were changed for a large dish of Peking duck bathed in a sweet plum sauce. This was followed by a dish of steamed white pomfret, laced with slices of ginger, red dates and fresh spring onions. Then there were bowls of pig's trotters and ginger, stewed in black vinegar and served with red eggs and slices of sweet ginger, symbolising the sweet and sour in life. The main dish of the feast was the suckling pig; one whole piglet per table, roasted crisp and red with its tail clothed in a pink rosette of crepe paper and served on a large white dish. The waitresses came round to each table to serve the guests a portion of the crisp skin and tender meat.

"Hmmm, very succulent, very good," the old uncle said approvingly.

"That's the way it should be; crisp and tender," said his wife, chewing on a juicy bit of meat herself.

"To be so tender, the piglet must not be more than two weeks old. When more than two weeks, the meat is tough," the gourmet-uncle said as he picked his teeth and sighed with satisfaction.

The meal ended with a warm dessert of sweet rice dumplings, delicately shaped into little balls of pink, green and yellow, swimming in a soup of sweet lotus to symbolise vitality and happiness, the marks of a good healthy life.

"Aiya, this Ah Yoong, where is she? I sent her to call Ah Kiong, and still she's not back!" Yee Mah turned to her son's father-in-law. "Chan-kah, please forgive my son. He's very badly brought up."

"Young masters of rich families all spoilt," the father-in-law replied, keeping his voice even so that there was hardly a trace of anger in it. He wiped his face with the hot towel which the waitress had just handed to him to mark the end of the feast.

"It's our daughter's fate," Siew Lai's mother said kindly. "You've been very kind to her, Yee Mah; she told me so herself. She says you want her to help you run the business. I hope our Siew Lai will be a good manager; she has a lot to learn."

Siew Lai's mother was secretly pleased that this ugly daughter of hers had so cleverly carved out a niche for herself. She had always advised her daughters to let the man come and go as he pleased. "Let him go freely," she had advised. "Just line your pouch with gold. Silver and gold are more lasting than a man's feelings." And like all housewives of her generation, she had her own secret hoard, accumulated through years of squirreling away money given by her husband for her housekeeping.

"Our Siew Lai has a lot to learn from you, Yee Mah. She's not very clever; please teach her," the mother continued with outward humility and inward pride. For a daughter-in-law to be made manager of the family business was no mean achievement.

"She'll learn fast, coming from our Chan-kah's family, for you have brought her up well," Yee Mah complimented her in-laws, relieved that they were not going to make a fuss over Ah Kiong's absence.

His absence, however, had not gone unnoticed by the other relations. Yoke-lin and Ah Jen at the next table had to listen to the comments of those relatives old enough to pass judgement on the young.

"That Ah Kiong is something else," said an old aunt. "An ingrate if you ask me. Ha! Not that I want to take sides, but tonight of all nights, he should at least come and give his mother some face."

"She refused to give him more money, I hear. That's why he's not here tonight!" another aunt reported.

"The world has changed! Everything can be bought, even a son's appearance!" an uncle laughed.

"I hear that rascal's got another woman outside. And he's not stupid, that Ah Kiong. Why should he come?" a third aunt asked, her eyes gleaming with mischief.

"What do you mean?"

Everyone round the table sat up. Nothing like a whiff of a scandal to spice a feast, especially a family gathering of this nature.

"Haven't you all heard?" The third aunt lowered her voice conspiratorially as she leaned across the table towards her audience, who shook their heads. "The medium of the Ninth Lord of the Heavens; never heard of him, mah?"

They shook their heads again. "Nah! Look over there! They say he helped Siew Lai beget a son. If our Ah Kiong doesn't come back, whose son is it, tell me," she whispered.

"Not so loud! Such things can happen, mah. The

Cowherd and the Seven Sisters, spirits and man ... " Another aunt pointed out.

"Right-lor! Some mediums are powerful. We don't know what happened. Yee Mah says this is her grandson. Who's to say no?" asked the old uncle.

"Chieh! Who's so stupid as to pull up her samfoo and show herself? If Yee Mah doesn't shout, and Siew Lai doesn't tell, what can anyone say?" the third aunt asked.

No one had any answer. Everyone stood up. The feast had ended, even though the rice ball dumplings had failed to sweeten the mouths and tongues of some guests. Yoke-lin felt a little sorry for Siew Lai. But what could she do, she thought. Being a much younger relation and one without the protection of a husband, and with the added disrepute of working in a cabaret, she could not speak without giving offence to the relatives, who might even ignore her. This possible loss of face and polite goodwill far outweighed her desire to speak her mind.

"Are you Miss Pang?" A neatly coiffeured woman of about fifty asked her. She was dressed in a matching dark blue samfoo suit and black court shoes. "I am Weng Chong's mother," she announced.

"Er, Mrs Lau, please call me Yoke-lin," she heard herself stammering.

"Forgive me, Madam Pang," the old lady sounded even more formal. "Please forgive me for speaking to you now. But I don't think the cabaret is where I want to go, I hope you understand?"

Yoke-lin nodded. A lady of her status would have considered the Green Parrot highly disreputable.

"Last night, Weng Chong spoke to me for the first time about you," Mrs Lau continued. "My son always tells me the truth. He wants to bring you home to meet me, his mother."

"I, er, I didn't know ..." Yoke-lin began but Mrs Lau stopped her.

"No, no, let me finish. Now other people do not see

things the way you and Weng Chong do. He is young, younger than you, right? So, you see, as his mother, I have to be very careful."

Mrs Lau's Cantonese was at its most polite and formal, and her tone was of one who was used to being obeyed.

"I will be frank and blunt, Madam Pang. People say bamboo must match bamboo, otherwise there will be trouble in a marriage. I'm not looking down on you. You have to earn your living. But when it comes to marriage, your background and Weng Chong's don't match. There will be problems. My son reads a lot of books, but life is not like in the books. It's not as if with love in your heart, plain water will satisfy your hunger."

Mrs Lau had not raised her voice but the guests and relations in the shop heard her. They gathered round like a crowd waiting for the storyteller to continue her tale.

"Mrs Lau, what is the trouble, ah?" Yee Mah called out in a voice loud enough to announce that, as far as she was concerned, she had nothing to hide from people.

"I'm so sorry to embarrass you, Yee Mah." Mrs Lau turned to her. "We've been neighbours these many years, and you know me, I don't like to cause anyone trouble. But this is about my son, Weng Chong, so I have to speak with Madam Pang here. She lives and works ... they are not places I want to go to," she said pointedly. "Yee Mah, you have a son, and I have a son, so you will understand how a mother feels. You chose your daughter-in-law very carefully. I too have a duty to protect the family's name. Weng Chong is the only son. How can I face my relations in this life and my ancestors in the next life, if I let him marry a cabaret woman? And one who has married before and is older than him? Yee Mah, I know she's your niece, but please understand a mother's feelings."

By now, Yoke-lin was sobbing, feeling utterly disgraced and ashamed.

"I have only one son. Doesn't every mother want to see her son marry well?" Mrs Lau appealed to everyone now, and there was no lack of sympathy for the widow. "He's all I've lived for all these years." She dabbed her eyes lightly with a beautifully embroidered handkerchief. "What else is there for me? My husband died when Weng Chong was born. Next month, my son will be going abroad to study. I don't want him to lose interest in his books and forget his duty."

"I understand, Mrs Lau, I understand," Yee Mah gently led her out of the shop. "We're neighbours, mah, we can talk things over. I'll speak to Yoke-lin. I give you my word, she will not see Weng Chong again," Yee Mah declared.

The guests and relatives followed them out of the shop. Yoke-lin was left alone. No one had spoken to her. Then Tai Ku came in followed by Ah Jen and Yenti.

"Aiya, my fate, my fate!" Tai Ku cried. "What else can I say? That I brought this shame to my own sister, on her grandson's first moon? Aiya, that I have travelled all the way from Ipoh to Penang to have my face torn off me, to let others ignore me, look past me! And all because of a daughter like you!"

"Grandmama! Grandmama!" Little Yenti was frightened.

"Don't grandmama me! Go to your mother!"

Tai Ku was fuming. She had never been so insulted in all her life, and in front of so many guests and relations. Where could she hide her face now? She might be poor, she raved, and her butcher-husband a nobody, but her sworn-sister - true, they were not related by blood, but still her sworn-sister - was the proprietor of a goldsmith shop, and she had always thought that the relationship would be enough to shield her, Tai Ku, from the shame of being poorer than the likes of Mrs Lau whom she had always been able to face as an equal before this. And the more she thought about the scene a moment ago, the more unbearable was her sense of shame, so that she could hardly breathe and was coughing and wheezing. The suspense was killing her, for what would Yee Mah do now? Tai Ku feared her sister's contempt more than anything else. That would cut off the source of whatever prestige she had gained among the tenants of Ming Sun Lane, none of whom had relations who owned a shop.

When Yee Mah returned, she found mother and daughter sobbing. Ah Yoong, who knew her old mistress well, said quickly, "Dry your tears, Tai Ku. Dry your tears, Yoke-lin. Auspicious day today, a happy day, ah, our young master's first moon!"

"Ah Yoong is right. Keep the candles burning, light more joss sticks. Aiya, really, choy, choy, choy! Bless us, ah, Goddess of Mercy! No crying, oi! Those who want to cry, cry elsewhere!"

Tai Ku dried her tears and followed her out of the room.

12

Two long and lonely months later, Yoke-lin received a large envelope. Inside was a cheque for two thousand dollars from Mrs Lau, and a poem written in Weng Chong's neat calligraphy.

"Who says my heart does not feel?
Grief has a life of its own.
Who is it, after all, that I am sending off?
How many days have we been with each other?
But at last, I know we can never swim
Against the tide of critical opinion;
How sad it is to be realistic."

She locked away the poem and did not speak to anyone about it. Then she tore up the cheque. However, she regretted it immediately for money was money, she thought, far more permanent than a lover's sighs.

13

Six months after Weng Chong left for England, Yoke-lin stopped going to the Green Parrot and coyly allowed Mr Lam to install her in a well-furnished room in a respectable tenement house where she was regarded as a favoured tenant by the landlady. She no longer seemed to mind that Mr Lam was twenty-five years her senior nor that his daughter was of her age, and even less that she felt nothing for him. It was enough that Mr Lam was providing her with the means to establish herself as a woman of substance with money in the bank and enough jewellery to dazzle the eyes of Tai Ku and Yee Mah.

The memory is a veritable store of facts, events and observations which the mind retrieves to toy and mould, sieve and weave into stories which we purvey as the substance of our history. Young and old, important or unimportant, we do it all the time, some more consciously and others less so.

In later years, when Yoke-lin was in her mellow fifties and the respectable wife of a millionaire businessman in Singapore, she used to tell the story of how, like the lotus in her name, she rose from the mud of humiliation to blossom and bloom, and proved her relations wrong, making them eat their hearts out that they had despised her.

By this time, with the confidence conferred upon her by wealth and experience, she could tell her story like a narrator blessed with the instinct and cunning of a rat catcher, luring her prey without seeming to do so, laying a piece of sausage here and a piece of cuttlefish there, advancing without any perceivable plan, without the slightest notion of structure or design to delineate fact from fiction.

She would interrupt her narrative flow to give her audience - mostly housewives who were fellow members of her Buddhist society - a list of all her grievances and sufferings to show how her faith in the Lord Buddha, in the Great Immortals, and in her own will and determination to change the course of fate, through prayer and meditation which she practised twice a day, had pulled her through. She would then digress into tirades against Tai Ku for having exploited her by living on her earnings, and harangue her listeners with a lengthy comparison between the treatment of her younger sister and herself. Ah Jen, in spite of all the benefits of parental affection and education, had become a compulsive gambler, which went to show - and here she paused, rolling her eyes heavenward - that fate could be changed and there was still some justice in this world. At this point, she would return to the beginning of her story about Ah Jen's wedding.

Tai Ku wanted a feast for ten tables of guests, that is, one hundred people, at a cost of one hundred and fifty dollars a table, and a roast suckling pig as the grand entree. It was Tai Ku's heartfelt desire, nursed through years of thwarted hopes and playing the sycophant to Yee Mah and her rich relations, to have the means to claim that although she, Tai Ku, was only the chief tenant in Ming Sun Lane, yet she had enough wealthy friends and relations to fill ten tables in Penang and Ipoh to celebrate the wedding of her youngest daughter.

It was the Chinatown syndrome - the poorer we are, the more we spend on weddings and funerals, often using borrowed funds, lest we lose both face and dream. The illusion of wealth and its attendant hopes and dreams is sweeter than the reality of poverty. And in this, the poor Chinese can understand more readily the Malay concept of a wedding as being "raja sa-hari", king for a day. Tai Ku dreamt of being a wealthy matriarch like Yee Mah, even if only for a day - Ah Jen's wedding day.

Throughout her life, she never gave up the hope of striking it rich, and saddled herself with tontines, chit fund contributions, mutual benefit and death benefit funds as well as the monthly lottery. It was hardly surprising that she had little money left at the end of each month.

"So my Tai Ku wanted ten tables," Yoke-lin continued. "In Yee Mah's goldsmith shop, she said, so that she could invite Yee Mah's relations, neighbours and workers, all the people she knew through Yee Mah." Yoke-lin paused and shook her head. "She thinks they're her friends. She doesn't know that such people talk to her just to give face to Yee Mah, not to her! Who knows Tai Ku without Yee Mah, you tell me? But never mind, I thought to myself, never mind. You want ten tables? You don't have the money, mah! So she tells me her problems, she calls me daughter. I listen. Now your Pang Yoke-lin here has become Tai Ku's beloved daughter again. Why? Because my purse is heavy now. She knows I have a soft heart. If you cry in front of me, I give you what you want! I'm like this; you all know me well. If my heart were hard, today I'd be as rich as my Yee Mah, not the poor woman you see in front of you!"

At this, her audience pooh-poohed her self-disparaging remarks while Yoke-lin, smiling indulgently, shook her head and protested.

"Aiya, you see me good and I see you good, right or not? We all have things to hide. Anyway, Tai Ku came to me because her sworn sister, that rich proprietress of the goldsmith shop, would not lend her that kind of money. Give her some? Don't even dream of it-lor! So when she needed money, Tai Ku hummed and hawed to me: only once in her life time, her last chance, the last daughter! She was old and getting on, and if for once, she told me, if only for once, she could hold her head high, she would close her eyes in peace, when the time came. So what to do? I looked at her. True, her hair was white. True too, I'm now rich. So, what's one or two thousand to me, right or not? She did bring me up, I thought; no matter that she ill-treated me, still I'm not ungrateful, and I pitied her. So I gave her the money. And not only that, I even bought her the jewellery she asked for. That's the way Tai Ku worked; give her an inch, she'd take a yard. You disobeyed her, she threatened suicide. Aiya, how many times I was forced to kowtow and beg for forgiveness! And what did she want the jewellery for? Not for herself! But for my sister, Ah Jen! For what would the in-laws think if her precious Ah Jen went over to them without a few pieces of gold? And then, the son-in-law is a government clerk. In Tai Ku's eyes that was a high post! Wah, working in the government-lor! So not good if Ah Jen were to be married to that clerk without some gold, mah!"

The sarcasm in Yoke-lin's voice was unmistakable, and the more she related the tale, the more excited she became so that her words rose and fell in a melodramatic rhythm reminiscent of the traditional storytellers in Chinatown.

"Tai Ku could lure a bird from the tree with her sweet words," Yoke-lin continued. "Ah Jen and I were two sisters, she said, and she treated us the same. Is not the palm and the back of the hand covered with the same flesh, she asked me? She would die in peace knowing that both her daughters - both, she said - are well-provided for. How much? I asked her straight. Oh, she hawed, she didn't know. But she was eyeing a diamond ring, five small diamonds shaped like a flower, just like the one Yee Mah gave Siew Lai, she said. Aaah, now you see what I mean? My Tai Ku is not stupid. But I'm also not stupid. I agreed immediately. But there was one condition, I told her. And that was that I be served the first cup of tea. Ha! I came first before Tai Ku, the mother, and Yee Mah, the aunt."

Once again, Yoke-lin paused to gauge the effect of her words. Like any good storyteller, she knew instinctively the value of the dramatic pause.

"What could Tai Ku say, you tell me?" Yoke-lin continued. "She needed my money to buy face. So she had to agree; what else could she do?" she laughed at the recollection of that sweet encounter with Tai Ku in which, for the first time, she had had the upper hand and relished the power that position gave her.

"That was the sweetest and costliest cup of tea I've ever drunk in my life! But it was worth every cent. Were the guests shocked? Aiya, how not to be shocked? Here was I, Jen's sister, the youngest of the relatives, ah, getting the bride's tea even before the bride's parents! Before the aunts and uncles older than me! Who had ever seen such a thing before at a wedding? It showed how much Tai Ku depended on my money. On that day, I don't have to tell you, every relation knew where Tai Ku's money came from.

Think about it. If I had waited my turn, like the filial daughter that I always was, why, I'd be the last to be served by Ah Jen. All the relations would have taken the tea and left. So, who'd be left to listen to me? I gave Tai Ku the thousands she asked for so I could have an audience. I held my cup in hand, and bit by bit, I told my story to the very same people who saw how that old Mrs Lau ripped off my face, and how Tai Ku and Yee Mah left me in the gutter! I who had worked all my life for her!

At twelve, I was sent out to wash dishes for a hawker. Then the Japanese came. I chopped wood and cut rubber in a factory. Tai Shook had no work. It was I who supported everyone during the war. Then at sixteen, she married me off. She said marry, and I married. I was that obedient, ah! After I was thrown out, I went home. Where else did she expect me to go? That's when she said no money for my baby daughter. She and Yee Mah ordered me to work in the Green Parrot. I worked, I obeyed, then what happened? Tai Ku took my money, all my earnings. On top of that, she said I brought her shame! Who can accuse me of being ungrateful? From that day, I told myself no need to be grateful any more! After the wedding, I never went back to Ipoh again!"

It was a tale of the tables turned and righteous vengeance. Yoke-lin, in later life, told her story like a true follower of those ancient heroes who could nurse an insult for a hundred years, high up in the solitary confinement of a mountain cave, in order to hone their deadly kung-fu skills and avenge themselves upon their enemy.

Yenti's Journal

When I was twenty-seven, I returned to Penang with Seng for our honeymoon. It was more than fifteen years since I had left the island. I wanted to show him all the places I had grown up in. I was idealistic then for I had wanted him to share more fully my life and feelings, the way I wanted to share his world. His English-speaking Baba family is so different from mine.

On the second day of our stay, we went to Temple Street. I was immensely pleased that the wet market was still there, older and more decrepit, but still standing like a grand old dame at the junction of Temple Street and Ah Kong Road. The hawkers lined the roadside as before. Chickens and ducks were slaughtered by the drain as before, plucked, cleaned and hooked up for sale all before your eyes. Seng turned away. He preferred the impersonal cleanliness of the supermarkets in Singapore. But I was pleased. The Cantonese grocers were still displaying strings of Chinese sausages, ham, waxed ducks, salted fish and packets of mushrooms and red dates, and the different grades of Chinese tea leaves in large wooden drums marked by red Chinese characters which Seng and I couldn't read. Except for the shops selling clothes, bags and household utensils, the market place was essentially the same. I sighed contentedly as I dragged Seng down the sidelanes and backlanes; a piece of my personal history was still here. But I don't think Seng understood my feelings that day. He kept asking me what it was that I found attractive about the wet market, and I couldn't put it into words. I would rather paint it.

Coming from Singapore where whole neighbourhoods could be demolished within three months and rebuilt within one year, this old sameness about the place struck Seng as 'backward', his very word, 'slow and undeveloped' And he would never want to live there. Anyway, I discovered that day that he had no sense of history, despite having spent part of his childhood in historical Malacca. Attuned to the future and the global city - that's Seng!

I listened to the past that day in Temple Street, retracing the things I had left behind, and I was dismayed when I came to Prosperity Goldsmith with its peeling paint and run-down look. Where was that facade of prosperity, the bright shop lamps, the well-stocked showcases, that aura of success? The sofa and the coffee table with the metal spittoon under it were still there, and so was the large black and white photograph of Yee Mah, above the mirror and the showcases. But some of these were empty and others were stocked with cheap-looking imitation pieces. The old man behind the counter glanced up. I asked for my grandaunt, Yee Mah. He looked puzzled at first until I pointed to the photograph above him. "Oh, wait-ah, wait, I'll call the old Tai-por. The old lady is very deaf, must shout to her," he said. And that was when I knew that Yee Mah's powers had declined with age and failure to keep up with the times. No one would have dared refer to her as the old lady in those days.

She was quite incoherent when I finally met her. She was only interested in telling me about her recent illness and hospitalisation, that the shop was her only means of livelihood, and that her only grandson was living with her. Beyond this, her mind wandered and she mistook me for someone else. According to the shop assistant, Siew Lai was away and Ah Kiong had left them. Her grandson helped out in the shop occasionally; he was running a dry goods store in the market.

I was surprised that the grandson had not amounted to much, that baby boy whose birth brought such high hopes and expectations. I asked to meet him, but he was too shy to come out to the shop front. Seng and I finally left.

Well, well, well, so what if one was born into wealth and privilege. I remember that that boy had an amah to look after him, a chauffeur to send him to school and several private tutors to coach him. And all that these accomplished was a storekeeper?

I felt maliciously gratified. At least, my mother and I had made something of our lives.

Child

"Give me a child
for the first six years,
and she will be mine
for the rest of her life."

Adapted from an old Jesuit saying

14

Five year old Yenti was sick with chicken pox and had to be confined to the cubicle. Feverish and irritable, she lay in bed, turning and tossing. Her face, arms and body were covered with the angry pink blisters which broke and itched, forming scabs she was not allowed to scratch. "Not if you don't want to be pock-marked," Aunty Jen said sternly. The girl shook her head impatiently. She was slight and rather small, like a brown sparrow, with dark eyes and a shock of black curls permed short because Aunty Jen, who was studying at an English-medium school, wanted her to look like little Shirley Temple. But the child was too young to appreciate her aunt's attempt to be modern. All she wanted now was her Grandma.

"Grandmama! Grandmama!" she cried.

"Sleep, Yenti, Grandpa'll tell you a story."

"No! I want my Grandmama!" the girl cried imperiously.

"She's just finishing the ironing. Grandpa'll fan you."

"No! I don't want! Tell Grandmama to come!"

"Oi! She wants you!" the grandfather, feeling rejected, shouted into the kitchen.

"I hear you! I'm not deaf. You think you're the only one living here, ah? Ah Por's grandson is sleeping next door!"

The grandmother bustled into the room with a bowl of hot soup, "for my precious," she exclaimed. "You people never listen. I say she's weak, the spirits will harm her, who believed me? See now she's sick. Last month sick, this month sick, who suffer? Me and her!"

The entire household had been revolving around the sick child, and the grandfather, feeling the heaviness of having failed to bring the child home from the playground before nightfall, left the cubicle without another word.

"Yenti, you naughty girl! Why do you shout so for Grandmama? Now you've made Grandpa angry. Grandmama has work to do!"

"I want to work with you," the child said.

"No, no, precious, you're sick, mah. Can't leave the room; you want someone to report to the police? Send you to hospital? Strangers mustn't see you like this," the grandmother was whispering. She was suspicious of all authorities in uniform. "Their spirits, ah, make you even more sick! Be good and stay here. Help Grandmama keep the evil spirits away, eh?"

The child nodded solemnly, not fully understanding but fully willing to conspire with her grandmother to keep at bay the evil that lurked everywhere after dark. To the child, her grandmother was the only one strong enough to protect her. But, the child thought proudly, her grandmother also needed her more than anyone else in the whole world. She was sure of this because her grandmother had told her so.

The child had a great capacity to listen and absorb the bits and pieces of the world that floated around her, twirling the seen and the heard round and round in her little mind till some sort of pattern emerged, rainbow-coloured, floating like the dust particles in the sunbeam, forming and re-forming, kaleidoscopic bits which she grasped in vain. Lying on her bed, her face frowning in concentration, she was absorbed in the timeless perplexity of childhood, trying to make sense of the adult world, fantasies and falsehoods fusing with reality.

The grandmother was ironing clothes in the warm airless cubicle. Her face was a constant grimace of pain from a gastric ulcer, disappointment and disillusion. Her cheeks a little sunken with age, her grey hair pulled back and knotted into a bun, and her large hands, so bony that the veins stood out, made the child's heart contract with love. It hurt the sensitive girl to hear her grandmother moaning daily that life had never been kind to her: she was always ill; Grandpa, a mere butcher, nothing but a butcher and a poor man, would never amount to anything; Grand-daunt Yee Mah would always look down upon them in her heart; Yoke-lin, the child's mother, never gave her enough money or appreciated her; Ah Jen, the child's aunt, knew only how to spend, not how to earn; and on and on. Yenti grew up with the idea that her grandmother had been done out of her rights, and that was why the poor old lady had to bend over her oil lamp and smoke home-made cigarettes.

"Those people think I like to smoke. I smoke to dull the pains in my stomach," the grandmother told the serious-looking girl. "I smoke so I don't feel the pain so much here." She jabbed her abdomen, and the child was vaguely annoyed at the other adults who could say such stupid things about her grandmother.

"When I grow up I'll buy you lots and lots of tobacco, Grandmama!"

"Aiya, Grandmama hopes you'll buy her more than tobacco! Buy me a big house, eh?" she teased, and laughed when the child nodded solemnly.

Every evening during the child's illness, the grandmother, a firm believer in the spirit world, brought in an earthen urn filled with red hot charcoal. From a biscuit tin she took out dried herbs, shavings of incense, camphor and sandalwood, which she sprinkled on to the charcoal, blowing until a smokey fragrance filled the room, driving out the evil spirits that might hurt the child.

Yenti loved the nights after nine o'clock when the landlady had switched off the mains, and the grandmother, like all the other tenants, had to light the oil lamps. Then, she had her Grandmama all to herself, for Grandpa did not live in the same cubicle with them. He lived in another tenement house because Grandmama did not want him to sleep in the same room with Aunty Jen who was a big girl now.

The grandmother lit the oil lamp, and smoked as she told stories of her life in China. At such times, her eyes had a faraway look as she spoke, and the child lying on the floor beside her, watched the huge shadows moving across the wall like warriors from the past in a Javanese shadow play.

"My father was a hard man," the grandmother said. "We girls worked very very hard, not like you so spoilt by Grandmama. Don't work hard, you'll be sold! My family didn't have enough to eat. Famine. Father sold us girls to feed the boys. I never saw my family again. That's why Grandmama didn't want to sell you. So sickly and troublesome, ah, but I clung to you. No, you cannot sell the piglet, I told your mother. I saved you. You're Grandmama's lifeline now. What else do I have?"

The girl hugged her Grandmama's bony chest, flat as a man's, and felt pity for the old woman.

"I'll look after you, Grandmama."

"That's what they all say. Your mother too wanted to look after me. Where's she now? How many times does she visit us, ah?"

The child was angry with the mother and this tiny seed sown in the night was cast into a dark corner of the child's heart.

Every afternoon, the child sat by the window, looking out for the grandfather pedalling up the road with a box filled with pork and strings of tripe. "Tai Shook! Tai Shook!" the women greeted him, and the child was proud of the grandfather whom everybody knew in Ming Sun Lane. "This is the butcher's granddaughter. Little girl, where's Grandpa?" they asked. The child's heart swelled with pride that she too was well-known because of her grandfather.

When she was well again, the grandfather took her

out each evening, sometimes to the park and sometimes to the clan association where she sat on his lap while he drank cups of hot tea and chatted with the other men. Sometimes, he took her to the Cantonese opera at the Great World Amusement Park. Seated on his shoulders, she was fascinated by the prancing warriors wielding spears and swords, and princesses in glittering costumes waving long white sleeves. Such things, however, must never be revealed to the grandmother, the child was told, because Grandmama would then take away the money for such outings from Grandpa.

"You and your Grandpa, go here, go there, and never tell me. Think I don't know, ah?" the grandmother complained. "Ha! A fly flits across my face, and I can tell straightaway whether it's male or female. You, Tai Shook! Don't take her to the back lanes and your dirty women, I tell you! If I find out, I won't just sit here. I'll break your bones, one by one, ah!"

And although the child cried, she did not reveal anything; and secretly, the grandfather was proud of his hold over the child too.

On the morning of her sixth birthday, Yenti was awakened by the grandmother. The sky outside was still dark and the oil lamp was lit. Aunty Jen began to dress her. She was sleepy.

"Stand still, Yenti. Move and move, how can I dress you?"

"I don't want to go!"

"What? Don't want to go to school? I told you, big girl now, must go to school," Aunty Jen was beginning to nag again. "1955, six years old, must go to school. I go to school every day."

"I don't want to go!" the child stamped her foot.

"Aiya, come to Grandmama. Don't make her cry this morning, Ah Jen. Very auspicious day! I will dress her, mah. Give me the ribbons." The grandmother parted the child's hair and tied two pink ribbons on either side of her head. "Nah, very pretty now. Your Grandmama can't read, can't write! In this world, ah, useless. You and Aunty Jen so lucky, can go to school! Next time, you can work and give Grandmama lots of money!"

The grandfather arrived and called out to them from the lane below. The three of them hurried down the stairs to join him in the dark streets. The grandfather was carrying an old-fashioned waxed paper lantern, the kind used by farmers to light their way through the dark country lanes in China. The lantern was a symbol of knowledge and learning, said the grandfather. "Yenti, big girl today; going to school! Walk in the light. Be bright, be clear. See the big characters on the lantern, eh? 'Kong Meng'! Ah Leong Sok says that means be bright and clever!"

The grandfather was in a happy mood, and although he did not express it in words, he felt that this was a new beginning for the family, his family. His granddaughter was going to school to learn to read the classics like scholars in the old days, and he was proudly leading his entourage to the Chinese school, a few streets away. Ah Jen was attending a foreign school teaching her foreign books and so, in Tai Shook's eyes, that did not count. He was not even sure whether the girl, now aged seventeen and in her last year of school, had ever learnt anything from those gwai-lo women who spoke a tongue utterly foreign to his ears. "The language of ghosts," he had called it when talking to his compatriots at the clan association. But since sending Ah Jen to an English-medium school was Tai Ku's decision, he had kept his opinions to himself while at home.

"Yenti will study the classics," Tai Ku was saying. "The three obediences and the four duties of a woman."

"Three obediences and four duties?" Tai Shook was puzzled.

"There! I always say you're an ignorant man. Never

heard of this, ah? You, Ah Jen, listen too. Don't say your mother never teach you next time. The Great Teacher said, ah, a woman, when at home, obeys father; when married, obeys husband; when widowed, obeys eldest son. Her four duties are to work hard, to submit, to endure and, er ... and, aiya, I forget the last one. So long, I've never recited this, I've forgotten already. Ask your teacher, Ah Jen."

"In the English school, we don't learn this, mah! We only learn English."

"I should have sent you to a Chinese school! But then people say English is very important. Next time you go out to work, you earn more."

"Then, Ma, why send Yenti to a Chinese school? That school is so old-fashioned," Ah Jen asked.

"Don't be stupid! This is the nearest school. The foreign school is so far away, who'll take her? If I have to take her every day, my old bones will break! And if I don't send her to school now, her mother will stop sending money and take her away. Then what? What are you going to eat?"

"I don't want to go! I don't want to leave you, Grandmama!" the child protested.

"Hush, you're not going anywhere. I will fight! Over my dead body, ah, if she wants to take you away from me! I'll tell your mother she can't disturb your study!"

The grandfather wanted no part in this struggle. He had no other motives except the secret pleasure of seeing his granddaughter attending a proper Chinese school with a teacher from his clan village near Canton, "a scholar well-versed in the classics", they had told him at the clan association. He himself did not know what the Chinese classics were but he had heard old men reciting, in a sing-song cadence, the verses passed down from generation to generation, and his heart had been filled with reverence.

"Clever girl, Yenti; next time, you read to Grandpa," Tai Shook patted the child's head.

"Aiya, don't talk so much. Hold up the lantern," Tai Ku hissed. "Now Yenti, you listen to Grandmama." She turned to the child and continued in a serious tone, "From today, your life will be lit by learning. They say the journey of a thousand li begins with the first step. Today, you're taking the first step. Work hard, listen to your teacher, and respect him like your father."

Tai Ku was reciting the phrases she had memorised for this morning's ritual walk, and wanted to impress upon everyone, especially the child, the significance of the journey so that no one could say that she was not teaching the girl anything.

The few people on the road, two betel-nut chewing Indian sweepers and an old man on a morning stroll, watched with curiosity the little procession going down the street. The dark sky was beginning to turn grey. The grandfather was carrying the lantern in one hand and leading the little girl by the other. Tai Ku and Ah Jen followed, each carrying a basket of food. The shuttered shophouses looked depressingly similar in the grey morning light in this poorer part of the town. There were the usual two-storey shophouses on both sides of the road with covered walkways down the row and broad pillars in front of the shops. Each pillar was painted with large red or black Chinese characters - Fook Onn Pawnshop, Pak Fook Tong Medical Hall, Yik Sang Tailor and so on - their names proclaiming the commercial dominance of two dialect groups, the Hakka and Cantonese, who had founded the town of Ipoh.

The school was a two-storey shophouse at the end of a row, and except for a blackwood sign board with Chinese characters in gold paint, there was little to indicate that this was a school. The grandmother knocked on the door. It was opened by a bespectacled man, a little stooped, dressed in white baggy pants and shirt.

"Good morning," he coughed politely.

"Yenti, kneel down and say good morning to Teacher," Tai Ku said.

"Good, good, get up, child, get up." The old man was beaming and bowing to the grandparents. New pupils were hard to come by these days for most parents were sending their children to the modern, government-funded schools.

"Teacher, please accept my granddaughter. She's very stupid. Teach her to be bright and clear. Beat her please, if she doesn't work hard," Tai Ku recited, having learnt those words for the ritual of begging a scholar to accept a pupil. Traditionally, it was right and proper for parents and grandparents to beg the teacher to mete out the necessary corporal punishment to make the child learn. Tradition had taught all right-minded parents not to spare the rod and spoil the child, and Tai Ku and Tai Shook, in retaining what little they had brought from the old country, took tradition seriously.

The teacher led them in. He was used to listening to such polite requests, muttered awkwardly by hawkers and tradesmen, who wanted a little learning for their children. But the teacher was growing old and tired. He had lost the revolutionary zeal of his youth which had made him come to the Nanyang to teach the children of his clansmen the wisdom of the sages. None of the children stayed long enough to read the elementary books, leaving school as soon as they could count a little and write their names legibly.

The school was just one big room with rows of desks and chairs. One half of the room was for the boys and the other half for the girls. Facing the class was the blackboard and the teacher's table. Everything looked old and worn-out, like the teacher. A film of chalk dust covered everything. At the back of the room was a portrait of Confucius in flowing robes, a clear sign that this was not the modern Chinese school advocated by progressive educators in China, hoping to pull the country into the world of science and technology. In all likelihood, this teacher of the classics had emigrated to the Nanyang to seek a safe haven, away from the upheavals in the old country.

"Kneel and kowtow to teacher, Yenti," the grandmother was saying.

"No need, no formality, please. This is where she sits," the teacher said.

"Please accept this basket, teacher," the grandmother bowed a little. "I hope you don't mind the small gift."

A boiled chicken, a large piece of roast pork, a roast duck and a packet of sweet sausages were handed to the teacher with a great show of thanking and protesting, of "too much, too much" and voluble apologies for "so very little, not much, we're poor people!" The other basket of cakes and sweets were for the pupils, to sweeten their mouths and their attitude towards the new pupil. Such gifts, while never a part of the traditional school fees, were often presented by people such as Tai Ku to show how precious their children were; the more precious the child, the more presents the family gave, even as they loudly begged the teacher to whip their precious ones to make them learn. It was permission granted by the left hand and taken away by the right.

"Come back soon, Grandmama!" Yenti shouted.

"Grandpa will fetch you at noon!"

School began each morning at seven. The boys and girls, ranging in age from six to fifteen, loudly recited their lessons in the same room while the teacher walked up and down between the rows of desks, a wooden ruler clasped behind him. The lessons were in Cantonese. The daily recitation over, the teacher wrote out the day's characters to be copied and memorised. The older pupils settled down to write each character into their exercise books twenty to thirty times, memorising all the strokes of each word. Then one by one, each went up to the teacher's desk to recite his lines. Yenti could never remember all her lines and was usually given a light knock on the head with a paper fan. But she enjoyed the calligraphy lessons. Every pupil had to practise one page of Chinese calligraphy every day, holding the brush perpendicular to the page, moving just the wrist, never the whole arm, an operation requiring a calm disposition, dexterity, and steady control of the hand muscles.

Once a week, the teacher told stories of hardworking and devoted mothers who gave up everything to bring up their children properly. Yenti enjoyed this part of school best of all, and remembered most vividly the story of Sum Leong, the widow who cut off the threads of her loom because her son wove a lie and laid waste her efforts to bring him up as an honourable man. When the story was performed as an opera, the grandmother took her to see it.

"See, ah! Remember it's me, not your mother, who gave up everything to bring you up properly! Your mother only gave money, I gave you my heart."

"You looked after me from small, very small, Grandmama?"

"Ha! From the time you were a tiny piglet! Day and night, you cried and cried, and I carried you," the grandmother said.

"Mother says she'll buy me toys in Penang."

"Aiya, you go for toys only and forget the one who brought you up single-handedly. You like those with money, eh? Grandmama is like the widow; no money! I only have my heart."

In the child's eyes, her grandmother was full of the drama of suffering and poverty, carrying in her pockets pawn tickets and crumpled medical bills. The old woman was often hunched over a pillow in gastric pain or railing at the ingratitude of those she had cared for, and at such times, her eyes were hard and bright, and the words gushed out like water from an unblocked drain. The child sat quietly, listening, storing all that she had heard and following the meandering course of her own childish imagination.

15

One year later, when Yenti was seven, her mother took her back to Penang Island to live with her. She was sent to the convent, an English medium school, and for the first time in her young life, she felt like a clod of earth. While other little girls chirped "Mary had a little lamb", she was dumb with shame. Few could understand her Cantonese rhymes. Of what good to her was her calligraphy and Cantonese operatic arias if none could understand her? The Primary One class in the convent was composed of Hokkien-Chinese, Tamil-Indians and Eurasians. All her teachers spoke English. She missed the applause and praise of her Grandmama. Each night, with her face turned to the wall, she cried herself to sleep.

The day her mother first caned her, for trying to run away back to Ipoh to look for her grandmother, little Yenti was absolutely convinced that Grandmama, who had never caned her, was the only one in the whole wide world who truly loved her. She had run as far as the end of the road before she was taken home by the neighbourhood trishaw rider. She had planned to roller skate all the way back to Ipoh once she had stowed away in the ferry. Yoke-lin cried bitterly as she caned her daughter, but the child remained unmoved.

From that day onwards, the neighbourhood trishaw man was engaged to send her to school and fetch her home to eliminate any chances of another attempt to escape. Lunch was usually on the table by the time she returned from school. But lunch was often a solitary meal, and the long hours from lunch till dinner were hours of solitary confinement in the cubicle she shared with her mother. Yoke-lin usually locked Yenti in the room while she was out playing mahjong, for she did not relish the idea of her daughter playing with the urchins of the tenement house. Yet at the same time, the mother found the hours with the child extremely boring.

At six o'clock each evening the mother returned dutifully to cook dinner for herself and her child, and that was the only meal that mother and daughter shared, eating in silence, concentrating on their own thoughts, ignoring the growing gulf between them.

Each night, at eight o'clock, Uncle Lam, the managing director of the Green Parrot Cabaret, arrived to take the mother out. And so after eight o'clock each night, the child was once again alone and locked in her room. Way past midnight, the mother would return, sometimes alone, sometimes with Uncle Lam. The child knew she was not expected to be awake at that hour, and she would pretend to be asleep, lying with her face turned to the wall, ignoring the noises she heard from the next bed till she fell asleep again.

In the morning, the child would awake to find that only her mother was sleeping in the next bed. It was much much later that the child realized that Uncle Lam, with a wife and children elsewhere, would never stay the whole night.

The child, however, never asked, never appeared to have noticed anything and the mother never explained.

Occasionally, the mother took the girl to the pictures. They would go in a trishaw with the man pedalling furiously, propelling their vehicle through the town's traffic. Inside the cinema, mother and daughter sat side by side, the child with a packet of sweets and the mother with a packet of sour mangoes. They seldom talked except in monosyllables. When the movie ended, the mother asked, "Tired?" The child nodded. The mother hailed a trishaw, and they went home.

When Yenti was twelve, it dawned on her that it must

be a lonely existence for her mother, who seemed to drift from day to day, playing mahjong and going to the pictures with friends during the day, and spending the evenings with Mr Lam.

That same year, Yenti visited her grandmother as usual during the school vacation. She took her grandmother the annual red packet from her mother. Unlike in other years, this year's red packet contained the small sum of fifty dollars only. Uncle Lam's business was failing and this was all that the mother could spare. The grandmother sniffed. "Humph! Staying one whole month and just fifty dollars? What can I buy with fifty dollars? You eat two or three durians and see a few shows and that will be the end of it! So clever, ah! No money, send the girl here for free! Rice costs money, ah!"

The grandmother became highly critical of her granddaughter's conduct. Yenti answered back a few times. There was a sharp exchange of retorts. The grandmother slapped her. Yenti was so incensed that she seized a bamboo pole and threatened to hit the grandmother with it. "You love money! You only want money!" she screamed. The grandmother swore and cursed. Yenti was sent home the next day, and that was the last time she saw her Grandmama.

Yenti's Journal

From the age of eleven, I knew we were getting poorer and poorer when Uncle Lam began to change his mode of transport. First he exchanged his white Mercedes for a small black Morris Minor; a year later, he rode a motor bike. He was already sixty then. After about six months, that brand new bike was exchanged for a dilapidated one that coughed and coughed like a tubercular patient and had to be pushed down the road before it could start.

His investments in two cargo ships had sunk in the South China Sea. Uncle Lam's bankruptcy broke Mother's heart and we moved into rented quarters and Mother took in boarders to support us. Once when I needed a mere three dollars for school fees, Mother had to empty my piggy bank. We counted out three dollars worth of ten-cent coins which Mother wrapped in a handkerchief, and I handed these to my teacher. Fortunately, Miss Lee, sensitive to my childish feelings, did not say a word. She took the coins and handed the handkerchief back to me. I do not forget such kind teachers.

Except for this instance, I don't remember feeling poor. However, poverty is relative, depending on what one has been used to and to whom one compares oneself. Mother felt poor because she had gotten used to being driven around in a Mercedes. To ride pillion on a motor bike after that must have seemed a terrible comedown. But I who had been ferried to and fro in a trishaw, and was never taken for drives in Uncle Lam's Mercedes, which was fortunate, did not miss what I had never had.

Mother and I could have survived with three bowls of rice a day on the income from the boarders, if she had been willing to accept financial hardship for the rest of her life. I suppose if there had been any love between her and Mr Lam, hardship would have been secondary. But where there is no love, money is primary, and that is my not-so-original observation of human behaviour. It was not that Mother was devoid of any feelings for Mr Lam, but after two years of washing and cooking for six college students, she must have had enough. She packed our bags one day, fostered me out to a family, and soon after left Penang for Singapore.

If I had dared to question her then, she would have slapped me hard. From young, Mother would brook no questions from me. I grew up silent in her shadow. For I was her burden. She loved and resented me. Her sense of responsibility for me far outweighed any pleasure she might have had in keeping me. "I must have done something in my past lives to inherit you in this life," she used to say.

Often I had seen her laughing and joking with friends at the mahjong table, making witty remarks and looking utterly relaxed. When she forgot about being mother, she looked all right, even pretty like any carefree girl. But when she saw me and was reminded of her maternal duties, the tension and rigidity returned to her face, making her stern and ugly.

I remember the large front room of the lodging house where Mother used to play mahjong. It was patronised by the Cantonese women who worked in the Green Parrot. The room had a red altar on which was the portrait of Kwan Koong, the red-faced God of War and Literature, holding a book in his right hand. Kwan Koong is the patron saint of the Cantonese who, on this basis, claimed cultural superiority over their traditional enemies, the Hakkas and the Hokkiens. Tua Pek Kong, the God of Wealth, is the patron saint of the Hokkiens. He is depicted as an old mandarin with a flowing beard, in gilt robes and holding a gold ingot in his right hand. "How crass!" the Cantonese sniffed. Fortunately, such dialectal rivalry is dying out with my grandmother's generation. Unlike Mother, I don't believe in the spiritual and medicinal value of joss stick ashes from the urns of the gods. But throughout my young life, I had drunk invigorating Chinese tea mixed with ashes instead of vitamin pills as my children do nowadays. I've always thought that if the Roman Catholics have raised ashes to the plane of ritual and meditation, contemplating the significance of Ash Wednesday and its profound message of "Dust thou art, and unto dust thou shalt return", then my grandmother had relegated ashes to the plane of the pragmatic and the medicinal in giving ashes a variety of utilitarian functions: ash to ward off evil, to cleanse the body and soul, to cure a fever and calm a palpitating heart.

I have digressed. I still have difficulty writing the way I feel about Mother. If she could be honest and admit that she hated hardship, and that that was the main reason she left Uncle Lam, I would have had no difficulty accepting her return to cabaret life. To hate hardship is no crime. Not a sin. But no, that would have been too trite a reason for Mother. She had returned to cabaret life for a nobler reason, namely me. She was not afraid of hardship, no, she said. "It was for your sake, not my sake, that I left Uncle Lam," she claims to this day. "He was old and had no money. He couldn't give you a better life and a higher education!"

"Why didn't you sell vegetables or something?" I had yelled back once. "Lots of women become amahs and hawkers. They managed to send their sons and daughters to university too!"

It was two months before Mother would speak to me again. The subject was never brought up again. And on my head sits the guilt of having been the sole cause of Mother's 'degradation', if one could call it such, since, like the Cantonese soap opera heroines, she had done it and everything else that followed, all in the line of maternal duty.

I don't know much about Mother's early years in Singapore. Nor when and how she met Ong Kim San, her next 'husband'. She had left me with a family in Kedah. It was three years later before I saw her again. By that time, she was expecting my step-brother, Ong Soo Beng, who was born soon after my arrival in Singapore.

Mother and Uncle Ong were proud and happy parents. Not that they hugged and kissed; they were restrained and circumspect in private and ostentatious only in public. They hosted a grand dinner at the Phoenix Restaurant for two hundred guests who feasted on roasted piglets, red eggs, sour ginger, and trotters stewed in sweet vinegar. Standard Cantonese fare predominated because of Mother's background, I suppose. After all, she was the one who had produced the son, and Uncle Ong had to respect her wishes.

Uncle Ong's First and Second Mother, the first and second wives of his millionaire father, gave the boy several gold trinkets which Mother proudly displayed in her room. These gifts symbolised the Ong family's acceptance of her, even though she was not legally married to Uncle. The birth of Soo Beng also benefited me. In recognition of Mother's accomplishment in giving him the longed-for son and thus enabling him to inherit a share of his father's fortune, Uncle Ong accepted me into his household. Today I address him as Pa, and he is the only father I have ever known.

As a young girl, I had resented my step-brother's importance in the household, and Mother's glowing pride in her darling boy. According to her, Soo Beng, the child of the gods, had brought wealth and harmony into the family. Well, Pa's business did prosper quite dramatically, but whether Soo Beng's birth had anything to do with it, only the gods at Ping Shan and Mother knew. I had had no part in their conspiracy!

Things are not always what they seem. Our household at the mansion was not always the quiet haven which Mother likes to portray whenever she speaks to the Buddhist Society. There were stormy times and ugly incidents before and after Soo Beng's birth. Snatches of conversation overheard and certain phrases stuck in my mind, stirring my interest in finding out about the "something more", as Pa called it, behind Soo Beng's birth. No one, however, would tell me more. Neither Mother nor her good friend, Yee Soh. The elders seldom think it necessary to explain or justify their actions to the young. It's either you know or you don't, and don't be rude; don't ask embarrassing questions. One learns a lot however by quietly listening to the adults when they forget one's presence. During my teen-age years, my imagination and fantasy were fed by the bits and pieces of conversation overheard, and so my fertile mind thinks it knows what happened between Mother and the medium of Ping Shan during her brief sojourn on that magical mountain.

Magic Mountain

"Such tricks hath secret desire
Where all is but dream and magic,
That if it would apprehend some joy,
In the night, imagining, some bringer of happiness,
How easy is a tinker supposed a prince!"

Adapted from "A Midsummer Night's Dream"
Shakespeare

16

The bedroom door upstairs opened, and Angela's high-pitched protest of "Aiya, don't-mah!" in Cantonese, was followed by a male guffaw that was hearty and satisfied. Yoke-lin, eaves-dropping in the kitchen, exchanged a knowing nod with her landlady, Yee Soh. She was the mummy of the Southern Cabaret where Yoke-lin had worked before she became Ong Kim San's mistress.

Then, the front door slammed, and Angela sauntered in. "Who was that?" Yoke-lin asked her fellow lodger. "Lucky, I didn't go into your room this morning."

"Aiya, just Old Teng," Angela yawned, adjusting the lace straps of her negligee, her dark nipples showing through the transparent apparel. She pushed back the thick black stresses falling about her shoulders with a gesture which hinted at the seductive powers of the twenty-year old and the high fees she could command. Young Cantonese women like Angela were popular in the fifties and sixties. "Ha! Our Cantonese mouths can out-talk all other mouths," Yee Soh used to say. "We can laugh and we can talk, chit-chit-chit all night! Squeeze us flat or puff us up, ah, we're flexible, not dead-set like the Hokkien girls. Ask them to sit, they sit. Stand, they stand. Stiff as a stick!" she sniffed.

Yee Soh was a warm cheerful soul of fifty or so, her age hidden behind thick powder and bright lipstick. "Sounds like Old Teng had a good time, if you ask me. Long time you kept him upstairs," she chuckled.

"Old Teng only comes for lunch time rest, mah. I keep him young, what!"

Angela reached for a rubber band on the table, and tied her tresses into a pony tail. With her hair out of the way, she looked like a young college student. And Yoke-lin realized with a sudden sinking feeling, that Angela's kind was her competition now. The young vixen who had stolen Ong Kim San's heart was probably, like Angela, in the full bloom of youth, and again like Angela, out to squeeze as much as she could from men addicted to the foibles of the flesh.

At thirty-two, nearly three years since she had left Penang to seek her fortune in the murky waters of a big city like Singapore, she was no longer as young or as confident of her powers to attract as when she had first stepped off the Malayan Railway. Slim and willowy then, she had been billed by the cabaret as an innocent arrival from up north, where the women were reputed to be less venal and more naive than the Singapore-born dance hostesses.

Now two and a half years later, and on the plump side, she had lost that freshness, although she was still an attractive woman with soft sensuous curves. Her lack of confidence in her own good looks, however, was betrayed in the sombre colours of her dress.

"How much are you getting out of Teng?" Yoke-lin asked.

"Not much, only about one thousand a month. Sometimes less. He doesn't come every time, mah!" Angela was giggling at her own clever pun. "Getting old-lor! Then his old wife watches him like a hawk, must go home every day for lunch. Except when he has a meeting, like just now!" Angela hooted.

"But one man like Teng, ah, is worth twenty other young ones. Old Teng wants secrecy so he's willing to pay," and Yee Soh's beady eyes brightened at the mental sums she was adding up for her new lodger. "Those young rakes give fifty dollars for one whole night! Expect the heavens to open up! You're only a few weeks here, and you've hooked Old Teng. He's very generous, one hundred an hour. Sometimes he leaves after half an hour! You listen to me, you can get even more out of him, ah!

Yee Soh's generosity with dollops of advice was legendary at the Southern, and this had often earned her large rewards whenever she had successfully matched the right girls with the right clients. The two jade bracelets gleaming on each wrist of her flabby arms were testimony to her success.

"I brought Old Teng to you so you can line your pockets a bit," Yee Soh was saying.

"I know, I know! I'll never forget your good deed!" Angela replied.

"Even if you want to go to Australia to marry Ah Alan, better fill your own pockets first. A full purse is better than a fool's heart, I say."

"Right, mah, but we people in love don't think like this. Alan and I, ah, together for years already. He trusts me and I trust him."

"Chieh! Love is one thing and trust is another. Love never fills anybody's stomach. You say Alan trusts you, then what are you doing behind his back? Yee Soh challenged the idealistic girl.

"But, but how else can I get this kind of money? Studying in Australia is very expensive, you know!" Angela protested.

"Ha! Men are not stupid. You think he doesn't know? Maybe, he wants the money so badly, he pretends not to know. But deep deep down, ah, they all prefer virgins when it comes to wives."

Angela, however, refused to be shaken.

"Aiya, Yee Soh, my Alan is not like that. We've lived together so many years already, I know him. He wants to be a dress designer. I asked him to go. Go, I said. I've two jobs, I told him, night clerk at the Southern."

Angela was giggling again, this time, over her own

deceit, and it sounded false, betraying the anxiety beneath the gay abandon.

Yoke-lin was sympathetic, seeing nothing wrong with Angela's bit of necessary deception. But how sad that even at the core of love and sacrifice, deceit was necessary to make the gift palatable. Had she not herself kept from Weng Chong her daughter's existence, just as she was holding back this same fact from Kim San now? Wait, wait a while more, she kept telling herself. With Kim San's eyes straying, how could she tell him that she had a fifteen year old girl in Malaysia, revealing her weak spot, the very thing he might seize upon to pry her loose. No man would want another's seed, Tai Ku had said, much less a grown-up girl. She should never have allowed duty to bind her so!

"Alan and I grew up poor," said Angela. "A bastard child, I was given to an old hag. I earned, she took. Alan was my first real friend. So I ran away with him. Seremban had no future for him. From a Chinese school and no Malay, what to do? But Alan's clever! He wants to do business, he says. I'll save, I told him, then we marry." Angela's eyes were full of the hopes of youth.

"Humph! Better not to put all your hopes on one man. You work like a dog here. Over there in Australia he mixes freely. All kinds of gwai-lo! He meets a girl better educated than you, then how? Where will you be? Never expect a man, ah, to be grateful forever. Water flows downhill, never up," Yee Soh continued to peck at the girl's confidence. "I've run this lodging house for years, ah! I've seen all sorts come and go. At the Southern, who doesn't know me, Madam Yee? I get people like you and Old Teng together, you benefit, ah, I benefit. Never depend on love. How much does it weigh? Look at Yoke-lin here. Two years wasted on Ong. Last night he didn't come back! See, what time now? Still not here!"

Yoke-lin glanced at the clock on the wall, her face

showing signs of stress and strain. Her dull eyes and the fine downward lines around her mouth gave her a pronounced look of discontentment which even her red lipstick could not hide. Half-past one, and there was still no sign of Kim San. This was another tell-tale sign that his feelings towards her had changed these past several months, for he used to be punctual, very punctual, and more often than not, in those heady days of passion, he was the one who waited while she completed her toilet.

"It's late, let's eat," she said.

"No, no, we wait. I'll drink coffee first." Angela waved a bejewelled hand in mild protest, setting the trinkets tingling, while in the other hand, she held her cup of coffee, delicately poised between lips and table, her little end finger sticking out affectedly. She had a way of tilting her chin and pouting those cherry lips whenever she spoke, which made old men like Teng indulge her like a child.

"I'll smoke then." Yoke-lin reached out for the pack of cigarettes on the table, her hand trembling a little.

"Aiya, Yoke-lin, so fast you smoke half a pack already. Bad for your health!"

"If I don't smoke, Yee Soh, my heart jumps." She got up and opened the window a little more. "So stuffy in here!" And she crushed the half-smoked cigarette in the ash tray.

"Sit down," Yee Soh said. "So impatient, what for? If he comes in now and sees your black face, sure to be another quarrel. And that's what the vixen wants, right? It's his birthday today, sure he'll come back, mah. You telephoned his office?"

Yoke-lin poured out another cup of coffee for herself. Dressed in a simple pink blouse and dark pants, she was looking more and more like the housewives in the neighbourhood with whom she played mahjong daily, now that she had stopped working at the cabaret.

The chime of the door bell brought her instantly to

her feet. "That must be him," and she hurried out to open the door.

"Aiya, Lau Ong, why so late? We're starving, ah! Your precious here, ah," Yee Soh was pointing to Yoke-lin, "has been waiting for you the whole morning."

"My apologies, Yee Soh, my apologies! Ah, Angela, you're joining us? Come, come, let's eat.

Ong Kim San, from Hokkien stock, was a stout man in his early forties, and blessed with the prominent paunch which many Chinese businessmen like him still considered a sign of good fortune. And indeed it was so in his case. His goldsmith shop in Chinatown was doing well, and he had just bought himself a new Mercedes like the one driven by his eldest brother and the richest of all the Ong brothers.

"Your new Mar-cee-dee must have cost you more than a hundred thousand, ah, Lau Ong! Maybe in the next life, I'll be reborn a man and make money like you," Yee Soh flattered him and put him in a good humour. This was a birthday meal after all, and whatever anger Yoke-lin might be feeling, this was certainly not the time and place to show it. Yee Soh's superstitious soul would not permit any unpleasantness to occur during a birthday meal.

Ong Kim San enjoyed the flattery and attention of women who could make what he considered witty remarks. He was relaxed and smiling as he turned to Yee Soh. "The Mercedes is a very good car. My friend gave me a good price."

Yee Soh and Angela fussed over him and plied him with question after question about the different makes of cars, both pleased that they knew how to make a man loosen his tongue and feel good about himself in such pleasant female company. The two of them, conniving and conspiring more by instinct than design, were subtly manipulating the drone who waxed eloquent in their midst, leading him on and affirming his belief in the superiority of his sex. What did they, mere women, know about cars and machines? Only men with an innate technical grasp of precision, science and mechanics could comprehend the finer points of car engineering, the brakes, the clutch, the suspension, speed and fuel consumption. Not that he, Kim San, was an expert, but he was a man and he had talked with other men who knew, and had acquainted himself with enough knowledge to surpass that of the women's.

His lucky star was rising at last after years of being in the shadow of his elder step-brothers, the sons of his father's first wife. Ten years ago, as a rebellious young man, he had left the wife chosen for him, and his father had threatened to cut him out of his will. But a year ago, on his deathbed, the irascible old man had relented and left him, the youngest son, with enough capital to start a goldsmith shop.

"We wish you a good year and a happy birthday! Good luck and good health!" Angela was giggling as she stood up and gave him a mock bow.

"Thank you, thank you! Come, come, let's eat," he laughed and sat down to a lunch of longevity noodles garnished with mushrooms, chicken, chopped spring onions and red chillies, painstakingly prepared by Yoke-lin.

"Hungry?" she asked as she sat down beside him. "Why so late?" She glanced at him but he did not offer any explanation for his absence the previous night or his lateness that day.

"I was entertaining your friend last night, Mr Teng," Ong Kim San said to Angela.

"Old Teng? Ha! He always talk business," she replied.

"That's why he's rich," Kim San said.

"Aiya, Lau Ong, ah, you're not so poor yourself! Come, give us a treat. Let's go and eat chillie crabs tonight."

"Another day, Yee Soh, another day. I have to meet some people tonight," and glancing at his watch, he rose from the table. "Don't wait up for me," he said to Yoke-lin. "Must work late tonight. Please excuse me, you all, ah, carry on eating. I've to return to my office now."

"But Mr Ong, you've hardly touched your noodles, ah!" Angela exclaimed.

"Never mind, never mind!"

Kim San was in such a hurry to leave that when Yoke-lin followed him out to the car, mute with disappointment, he did not even pause to say goodbye.

"Don't be too late!" she shouted. But her words were drowned by the roar of the car's engine. He drove away without another glance at her.

Back in the house, Yee Soh was ready with some advice. "If I were you, ah, I'd tail him. See where he goes."

"I did, Yee Soh. Three nights I followed him. Three nights he was at that Forest Lane flat."

"Aaah, you're not so stupid then," Yee Soh murmured and wiped her mouth. "Very good noodles."

"Sometimes, I feel like rushing into that flat with a chopper. Kill him and then kill myself and put an end to this pain!" Yoke-lin's eyes were reddening again. She made an effort to control herself but the past year weighed upon her like a millstone. "He changed when he got that inheritance. Remember? He was poor when we first met. Only I, ah, Pang Yoke-lin, didn't look down on him at the cabaret. Who knew him at the Southern then? Now suddenly, he's got so many friends. Dinner every night outside! For the past three months, I can count on my fingers the nights he's come back to me!"

She could not finish the meal. And now that she had started to say what she had hidden in her heart these past twelve months, she could not stop talking. It was as if a dam had been breached and the waters released.

"He's changed! Not like his old self any more! He used to talk and joke a lot. You heard him, didn't you? Always coming here, always making us laugh and taking us out! Now, ah? Don't even think about it! Look at him, like a big lord, he comes, he goes! I can't even get a word out of him! Last week I asked him. Where did you go? Where did you spend the night? No answer. Not a word! He kept quiet. Lay on the bed, eyes closed. Didn't even look at me. This is the third time this week you didn't come home, I said. Even Buddha will fly into a temper, I said. You think I don't know where you went? You think I'm blind, I asked him. The walls have ears, I said. And people have mouths. You go to that kind of house, high-class, yes, but you'll still catch a disease, I told him. He got up. Didn't want to listen anymore, and just left! Didn't come back for a week! Remember? And tonight, see-ah! He won't come back!"

She choked back her tears for she hated to cry in front of others. What could other people do but shake their heads and cluck sympathetically. The thought of losing out to another woman, younger and more attractive than herself, and able to get more out of Kim San now that he had grown prosperous, seemed like a gross injustice and betrayal of all her hopes. She had settled on him when he had no shop to speak of, having resigned herself to being tied to a man without too much money, willing to settle for less and giving up all hopes of ever becoming wealthy like Yee Soh. She knew she had passed the stage of youthfulness and all she asked for was a home, a family and three bowls of rice a day, she confessed to her audience. Would they say she was ambitious? A climber? All she'd struggled for was a home with a man she could call her own. Not shared with another woman! Not for her the diamonds and gold she saw on others, just a family and home of her own.

What she did not tell her audience was that, eating her heart out, was the news that Ah Jen, the sister married to a mere clerk, had bought a house in Ipoh while she, Yoke-lin, was still renting a room in a lodging house. For months, she had been scheming to get Kim San to buy her a house. That she had failed to do so was yet another thorn in her side. Her greatest fear was that this vixen might succeed where she had failed.

"You see for yourself, Yee Soh, what an ingrate he is!"

"People change," her landlady replied, "especially men."

"Sometimes I think of going back to the Southern, earn my own living again."

"Yoke-lin, ah, be realistic. I speak frankly. The young chicks these days, not like you and me. They can fat-fat in English, dance a-go-go, all very modern! You can't compete. Women our age, ah, must quickly find a man and settle down."

Yee Soh's response stung her to the quick. At thirty-two, she was already seen as middle-aged and past the time when men would gladly pay for an hour of her company.

"All men are like this, only want the young ones," Yee Soh said.

"What can I do? Tell me what to do," Yoke-lin sniffed, stifling the sob that rose in that slender throat which Kim San once loved to stroke.

"If I were you, ah, I'd have a baby. A son. A man like Kim San, more than forty already, he'll want a son. Don't forget Ong Bus Company is still in the family. The estate is not divided yet because his First Mother is still alive. And she controls the company through her eldest son, I hear. But when she passes away, sons and grandsons will have shares. If Kim San has no son, he'll lose out to those who have.

"How do you know all these things?" asked Angela.

"Chieh! No secret, mah! Lau Ong's father was an old tortoise, one woman after another! Who doesn't know about him? He was a big man. Even those in Hongkong and Indonesia knew. And the old man liked to talk big after a few drinks. I, er, in my younger days, used to go out with him," Yee Soh smiled coyly. "But don't tell Lau Ong; not nice. The old tortoise helped me buy this house."

Yee Soh, refusing to dwell on her past, quickly returned to the subject of bearing a son, urging Yoke-lin to consider it.

"Not that I haven't, Yee Soh. I've been to many doctors, ah."

"What do they say? Something wrong with you?"

"No, nothing wrong, they said. The last one was Dr Tan. He asked me to take Kim San to see him. But he won't go!"

"Then, something wrong with him," Yee Soh said.

"Don't know, but he always says, wait, wait, when I talk about family."

"If I were you, I wouldn't wait. He's got a shop and money now. If you don't get him, others will, and then too late already! Once there's a baby, a bit more difficult for him to leave unless he's very very heartless. With a baby, ah, especially a son, you've got claims. And anyway, two years already you're with him, time enough you get something more from him. Something solid," Yee Soh urged. "Look at me, a poor bar girl last time. But I was slim and quite good-looking then." Yee Soh put two arms round her own waist to show her audience the expanse of her girth and laughed now that her body occupied the entire space of a large armchair. The diamond rings glittering on her pudgy fingers could not be taken off. "Too fat now," she sighed. "When I die they'll have to chop off my fingers to take off the rings!"

Yoke-lin did not disagree with Yee Soh's advice. It was sound. It was sensible, and the only way out for her, she felt. Yet she was deeply irked by the unfairness of it all, a deep sense of injustice for which she had no words. If she had had an education, she would have protested against it. Why should life or fate afford a woman only her youth and good looks as the sole avenue to the acquisition of a permanent relationship with a man? Something was not right. Why should men appreciate like vintage wines, the older the higher their market value, especially men who came packaged in a profession with a high income? But the reverse was true of women. They depreciated with the years like roses that fade. If she were educated, she would be a lawyer and be single and live an independent life, she thought. She would free her daughter, Yenti, and send her to university, she vowed silently.

Angela, who had been silent all this while, spoke at last. "Ha! That's why I want to marry fast when I'm young," she exclaimed. "Who wants to marry me when I'm old? You think I don't worry about Alan? Day and night I worry! What if he meets someone better? Educated? You think I like this life? The wives curse me daily. Old Mrs Teng is one. But I don't snatch the husbands! They come to me! I sell, they buy! It's honest; I don't steal, I don't cheat! It's my own body, what! You sell! I sell! Let's see who buys? Right? Don't say I'm not a friend, ah, Yoke-lin. I'm in a difficult position. Kim San's new woman is my friend too. But I don't want trouble, see? She's very keen, ah! Tonight Old Teng and I are supping with them, midnight, Bugis Street! Her name is Anna."

Angela gathered her things and went upstairs without another word.

Yoke-lin appealed to Yee Soh.

"Aiya, very competitive in the cabaret, friend or no friend," the mummy sighed. "I'll go with you tonight."

17

To those interested in the minutiae of local history, Bugis Street is the only reminder of our link to the fierce warriors, skilled seamen and shrewd traders, the Bugis of the Celebes, who set sail from the port of Macassar in the seventeenth century, and hired themselves out to troubled sultanates like Johore, Kedah and Perak. Mercenaries are the prostitutes of war who sell their warring skills to those willing and able to pay the price. It is one of the overlooked "little ironies of Singapore" that those who ply the flesh trade, purvey erotica and prostitute their sensuality should congregate in Bugis Street. But it is doubtful that the Chinese, Indian and Eurasian pimps, prostitutes and transvestites and their clientele are aware of their historic link to such an illustrious past. To the foreign visitor from the West, the name of "Bugis Street" today evokes the mystique of Singapore's supply of oriental exotica, exciting the fantasies, suppressed by the sobriety of their own domestic lives back home. The Bugis Street of the fifties and sixties - before its demise at the hands of moral hygienists, and rather surprising resurrection several years later - was what Soho is to the young Singaporean visiting London for the first time, freed from parental restraint. To the foreign sailor, tinker and soldier as well as local gourmets and roamers of the night, Bugis Street was a parade and carnival of exotic food and faces.

Twenty to thirty food stalls lining both sides of the narrow road changed the busy thoroughfare by day into an open-air gourmets' paradise by night. Slabs of roast pork, pork ribs, slivers of pig liver, long strings of red sausages, brown tripe, long slender slices of raw beef, strips of white fish, fish roe, whole ducks and chickens and bundles of greens hung from large metal hooks fixed to the wooden beams stretched across the stalls, and everything was brilliantly lit by naked bulbs strung across long wires.

The mood of the throng milling around the stalls at midnight was carefree, jovial, curious, eager, expectant and restless. They were looking for something to tease the palate, fill the stomach and soothe the tired nerves: a bowl of turtle soup perhaps, a plate of fried frog's legs, or a cup of snake's blood to stir the passions. The people ate and drank, talking and laughing as if tomorrow's workaday sun would never rise.

"You know, ah, this place will go soon?" Yee Soh observed. "The man who sells turtle soup told me the gov'ment wants to move them. When the time comes, he'll retire, he says. He said these people only think about whether a place is clean or not clean," Yee Soh continued as they looked for a place to sit.

"This gov'ment is strict," Yoke-lin muttered. She was not really interested in the hawkers' problems right now.

"Aiya, if not strict, the people won't listen! No fines they spit. Got fines, they don't spit and throw rubbish here and there! If no fines, ah, you talk till your throat dries up, no one will listen!"

They found a wooden table and sat down next to a dirty lorry covered with clumps of earth, parked at the roadside for the night. The dark drain running alongside it oozed with sludge and it wouldn't have surprised Yoke-lin, who grew up in just such a neighbourhood, to see dark furry creatures scuttling in that drain. But people who ate at roadside stalls were seldom preoccupied with such details, at least not at midnight when other priorities like what to eat and where to sit to get the best view of the parade of transvestites, had to be considered.

People sat everywhere; on wooden stools around rough wooden tables, on stools in the covered walkways of shops closed for the night, tucked behind broad stone pillars, between the narrow confines of passageways, between the food stalls, next to the drains, beside the parked cars and lorries, and under the street lamps with flying ants buzzing around and falling into the soup.

The cinemas and cabarets, having closed for the night, had disgorged their cabaret dancers, bar girls, massage parlour girls, mistresses and constant companions of one kind or another, men dressed as women and women dressed as men. From midnight to three o'clock in the morning, people were sauntering, eating and drinking with their patrons, clients, friends and lovers till all heads were turned to gaze after eight young 'women' in red and black taffeta gowns. Those fair damsels held up their satin fans, smiling and bowing to the cheers and catcalls of the crowd, their eyes inviting, their fair shoulders and plunging necklines alluring. A group of white Americans clapped and hooted while another bunch of tourists, some Japanese, even stood up on their stools to get a better view. And a few bold ones posed with the 'ladies'. The lights flashed and the cameras clicked. Then the enterprising pedlars came up to the tourists with the instant photographs, and the men, laughing, paid up and passed the souvenirs around.

"That's twenty dollars for one photo of those ah quas," Yee Soh complained. "Like this, the men will spend their money like water."

"Beer, cigarettes, women and gambling, they're willing to spend," Yoke-lin added.

And the two women grumbled about their men and their women as if they themselves were not part of the conundrum of human sexuality and its multifarious expressions.

The waiters in white singlets with white 'Good Morning' towels flung across their shoulders called to the tourists, "Sir, sir, dis way! Hey, velly good seafood! Here come! Come! Dis way, dis way!"

At the table next to Yoke-lin's, a young Chinese male in black shirt and white trousers and sporting a thick gold bracelet, was showing a party of Indian men some photographs. The Indians with greasy hair smelling of pomade and conservatively dressed in long-sleeved shirts with bright cuff links of imitation gems, smiled and shook their heads. But the Chinese pedlar was persistent. "Chakap-lah! Chakap! Berapa? How much, you say-lah!"

At the table just in front was a stout middle-aged Chinese man guzzling a bowl of steaming noodles while his young companion was solicitously dabbing the beads of perspiration oozing from his flushed face.

"See, ah," Yee Soh was whispering, "men like to be pampered. Look at Angela; young vixens like her know how to do it. Then those who don't, like Lily Chan, they go, ah, to mediums. Cast a spell over the man. Charms, amulets. You know Lily Chan?"

Yoke-lin shook her head.

"That's the one I told you who got the lawyer. That's why I keep saying, go to Master Loong. He's not cheap but very good. But let's order our food first."

A waiter came and Yee Soh ordered noodles fried with chicken and abalone, and a dish of vegetables sauteed in oyster sauce.

Yee Soh continued, "The lawyer, very clever and rich, wanted to return to his family. Afraid of scandal. But Lily, ah, is very strong, very determined. Two years as his mistress, you think Lily will let him go?"

"What did she do?"

"She went to Thailand, saw a powerful medium. I heard the medium gave her a special bath."

"He bathed her?" Yoke-lin could not believe her ears.

"Ya, bathed her and gave her a bottle of holy water. After the lawyer drank it, he left with Lily for Hongkong. If you don't believe me, ah, ask Lucy Leong."

The waiter brought a pot of tea and a large china

bowl with four small teacups without any handles. Another waiter brought a kettle of hot water which he poured into the large bowl. Yee Soh took out two pairs of wooden chopsticks from the metal container in the centre of the table and handed a pair to Yoke-lin.

"This China tea, Goddess of Mercy brand, very good for the throat," Yee Soh was saying as she fished out two teacups with her chopsticks. "I like the stalls here. They give you teacups, not glasses."

Their food came and the waiter, having given the table a cursory wipe, collected his bill and gave his sweaty forehead a wipe with the same 'Good Morning' towel, and withdrew.

"Yee Soh, I've been thinking," Yoke-lin began. "Kim San's manner has been very strange for several months. He looks past me, not a word out of him for days. Then when he comes home, very late, and by that time you're at the Southern. He just sits and eats. Doesn't talk. Like, like he's waiting, always glancing at the clock. Then nine o'clock only, ah, he goes upstairs, bathes and changes. Then he leaves. He doesn't care what I say. I ask, what time you're coming back? He mumbles like he's got something in his throat. You think the vixen could've given him something to drink?"

"This kind of thing hard to say, mah! Better see a medium like I told you. Look at him this morning! His birthday, and he went off like he got something to hide!"

"You're my witness, Yee Soh. Since I stopped working, I've not met another man. I'm not like other women, eat with both sides of my mouth..." she paused for her voice was beginning to choke again at the thought of what she could have gained if she had been less faithful, less foolishly faithful.

"This world, ah, dog eats dog. You don't do it, others will and in the end you lose out. The other woman will get

Kim San if you don't do something," Yee Soh warned her again.

Yoke-lin put down her chopsticks and took a sip of the hot tea. She could not eat. Her eyes were on the far end of the road. Kim San and his woman should be coming soon. It was already one o'clock in the morning. What wrong had she done to deserve this, she asked Yee Soh, and sighed. What?

He came home with his dirty clothes and took away the clean shirts and trousers she had ironed. Did she complain? Even now, she was looking after him like a proper wife while he treated her room as a laundry service. She didn't live for his money alone. She had always thought that they would have a house and family later. Later, always later, those were his words. And she had listened. Why? Because he said he wanted to build up his business first. She was not the one who was ambitious. If there was rice she would eat rice. If there was only porridge, she would eat porridge.

She called upon her landlady to be her witness, not that she wanted to praise herself, she said. Kim San had been a nobody when they first rented the room in Yee Soh's lodging house. Now he had a shop, a new car and a few thousand in the bank, and he thought he could cast her aside! She'd given him her youth! The ingrate! She could have found someone richer if he had not come along, day and night, day and night, begging her! So, she'd said to herself, here's a good man who cares for you; settle down and have a home.

If she were educated and knew how to read and write, she'd work in an office. Who wouldn't want such a life? Which woman wanted to depend on a man and have to kowtow once he'd tired of her! She called upon her companion to be the witness again. Was it not true that when Kim San opened his shop, she'd been the one who had saved every cent she could out of her housekeeping to help him? True, the money came from the sums he gave her each month; but it was not as if he gave her thousands, yet she'd managed to save. She ate poorly at home so he could eat well outside and entertain business associates. Such dinners counted in Singapore, she said. If others thought highly of you and you acted rich, they'd trust you a bit more. Who'd trust a poor man, right or not?

The more she talked the angrier she became, for her sacrifices had not been rewarded with something solid like a house, which would have been a consolation even if Kim San's feelings changed. She was a fool, she said, to trust his affection. She had thought only of him and nothing about herself. When he had wanted to play mahjong, she played mahjong; reared fishes, she reared fishes too and even washed the tanks! What more did he want? On and on, she talked, drinking one cup of tea after another.

Yee Soh signalled the waiter to bring another pot. Yoke-lin picked up her chopsticks. But she put them down immediately. Coming down the far end of Bugis Street was Kim San with a young, cheongsam-clad woman clinging to his arm. Next to them was Angela holding the hand of an elderly man.

"That's Ruby Tang," Yee Soh said. "The old man with Angela, ah, is Old Teng. He owns Fook Onn Goldsmith."

Even from a distance, it was painfully obvious to Yoke-lin that Kim San was enjoying the woman's chatter. One hand held on to Kim San possessively while the other waved animatedly, pointing to this and that stall. Yoke-lin's eyes strained after them as they weaved in and out of the crowd, the figures of men and women blocking them from her view. She would have given chase, but as in a nightmare, her body would not budge.

The incessant chatter about her grew louder and louder, the hissing and buzzing increased as human voices receded, becoming indistinct till only a cacophony of inhuman hisses swarmed about her ears. The people on her right and on her left were chewing noisily, masticating greedily like beasts. The blood rushed through her veins like a tidal wave. She tried to reach for her cup of tea. It fell from her hand and hot tea cascaded on to her. Hastily she stood up. Should she march up to the couple and scratch the vixen's face? Tear off that smug smile?

"Yoke-lin, Yoke-lin, sit down," she heard Yee Soh calling from a distance. "Don't do anything foolish. Let them be, ah! Lose tonight. Fight tomorrow and win!"

18

The medium of the Temple of the Eight Immortals was having a solitary supper in the secluded kitchen, screened off from the main courtyard by a wall with the traditional moongate as its doorway. He took quick sips of his hot tea and dipped his chopsticks into the bowl of rice porridge and salted eggs in much the same way as his immigrant forefathers had done, crouching on the bench like the trishaw riders in Chinatown.

His lean brown face was that of a manual labourer used to working long hours in the sun. The Japanese Occupation had left its scars on him. When he was just a boy in his teens, he had been caught, tortured, charged with the crime of being a courier for the British forces, and sent to work on the railways in Thailand. He seldom spoke of his past, maintaining a silence which intrigued his more garrulous devotees and sparking off stories which he neither denied nor confirmed.

One story was that he had run away from his home in the mountains of Southern China when he discovered that he was the illegitimate offspring of a renegade monk and his housekeeper. The truth, however, was more mundane. He had run away from a small village in a rubber plantation, and made his way to Kuala Lumpur, where he had fallen in with a gang of 'jaga kereta' boys, harrassing drivers to let them guard their cars for ten cents. Drivers who refused had found their cars scratched and tyres slashed.

A few years later, the street urchin was recruited into the White Crane Secret Society to work as one of their warriors, protecting the rich Chinese towkays who had to drive up and down the lonely trunk roads of the Malay

Peninsula whenever they visited their tin mines and rubber estates. But before long, he was wanted by the law and had to go into hiding. Some said that he had killed a towkay for the sake of a young girl who had ensnared his heart. Others maintained that he had been involved in the then lucrative opium trade through the mistress of the Big Boss of the Yellow Flag. He was known to have a weakness for rich women.

But the more devout of his followers believed that it was a vision of his dying father, the monk of Ping Shan, which had sent him hurrying back to the temple where father and son were eventually reconciled. The dying monk from Southern China was said to have taught his son the sutras of the Eight Immortals, and passed on to him the secrets of the I-Ching and Pak-Kua. But how Master Loong - a name which he wore like a monk's robe, to be taken off whenever he liked - came to be involved in the affairs of the Temple of the Eight Immortals in Singapore, under the protection of Mr Charlie Wong and the patronage of Mrs Chan Siew Lai, the new proprietor of Prosperity Goldsmith in Penang, was something no one knew and no one cared to find out.

Mr Charlie Wong was the big boss of the secret society that protected Chinatown's hawkers, shopkeepers and operators of opium dens, gambling houses, hairdressing salons, massage parlours and houses of prostitution. Only the foolish and the foolhardy would dare incur the wrath of Mr Charlie Wong and his chief bodyguard, Big Tree Log.

To his devotees Master Loong was a kind and vigorous man of fifty or thereabouts. But like all traditional Chinese, he never revealed his age. He was proud of his vigour and what he liked to call his iron constitution. "Not a day ill in bed in the last twenty years", he told his followers, the wives of clerks and salesmen, when he was encouraging them to exercise and to do Taiji. "It gives you inner strength and keeps you young. Look at me." The simple housewives laughed, glad that he was still interested in them despite being courted by his wealthier and more demanding followers, the wives of traders and proprietors.

Master Loong was venerated in much the same way that the ignorant and the superstitious worship the avatars, beings believed to have descended from Heaven to help ordinary people on earth. Some had likened him to the Immortal Beggar Monk who could cure the sick with miraculous pills made from pellets of dirt rubbed off his body. Others believed he was the reincarnation of the holy monk of Ping Shan, believed to be his father.

They saw him through the lenses of superstition worn by those desperately in need of hope in a world in which they were perpetually poor and suffering. Women came to him when husbands deserted them, when mothers-in-law ill-treated them, when relatives looked down upon them and spoke ill of them, when family businesses were failing, when there was not enough rice in the rice bin or not enough money to buy a coffin and bury a parent. Master Loong listened, counselled, consoled and comforted, sometimes curing their aches and pains, reducing their anxieties and unhappiness, restoring their confidence, and gave them hope for a better life to come.

If at times, some felt his cures to be strange and unorthodox, they regarded them as the prerogative of his special calling. "Never walk past a fire hydrant if you want to bear your husband a son," he told one despairing woman. She did as he instructed, and within one year gave birth to a healthy boy. Such success stories, circulating among the residents of Chinatown, had won him many devotees. "Our sorrows are the sins of past lives," he told his followers. "The little good we do in this life will bring us a better life next time." And the wealthy among his devotees dipped into their pockets and contributed generously to the temple's building fund, much like the parishioners of a church responding to their pastor's appeal for tithes.

While the modern evangelist might use the tools of mass media to spread his message, the temple medium uses the past, brought over from a China belonging to a long lost time when ghosts, demons and gods were woven into the fabric of daily life. It was mysterious and reassuring that through this representative of the gods, one could appeal, cajole, buy or bribe one's way to happiness in much the same way that wealthy Catholics, before the Reformation, used to buy indulgences.

"Accept your fate. The gods know best; leave your life in their hands," Master Loong said whenever he had no answer to human suffering. In such moments, the gleam of pain in his keen dark eyes and the long strands of hair he sported at the temples, gave him the distinctive simian look of a shrewd, ageless gibbon, like the legendary Monkey King who defied the Jade Emperor and stole the peach of longevity.

"Master Loong!" exclaimed Siew Lai as she came through the moongate and her tubby body waddled up the kitchen steps. Puffing and out of breath, she sat down beside him and fanned herself with a large white handkerchief, like a Teochew opera actress. "Aiya, my heart!" she panted. "I looked everywhere for you. I didn't know you were hiding here!"

She rubbed the large mole on the right side of her nose. Twelve years of unhappy marriage had driven this matron to devote herself to mediums and temples, to ensure a better next-life while adding a much needed distraction to an otherwise boring present. The birth of a son had given her financial security and the brashness of a woman of substance. As the proprietor of Prosperity Goldsmith since the death of Yee Mah, she lived a life of relative ease, if not a happy one. Her husband, Ah Kiong, had left home many years ago, but then she herself was seldon home. She had followed Master Loong from town to town, up and down the peninsula, wherever he went to conduct temple services. To everybody, she was his financial manager. "He has no head for money. If I don't look after him, he'll have nothing to eat next time," she declared, and took charge of him.

Human relationships being fluid as the sea itself, over the years there had formed between the medium and his devotee a complex bond of mutual exploitation, both physical and mental, earthy and sublime, which a simple label like 'mistress' cannot encompass.

"How did you get here?" Master Loong asked, making no attempt to hide the irritation in his voice. He wished she would leave him alone sometimes. The years had made him weary of her.

"Charlie Wong drove me all the way from Penang. You're so busy, ah? No time to phone me? I waited so long, still no call. So I came!"

"I didn't know you were waiting for me to phone," he said sullenly.

"All these years, you know me well enough, mah! No need to tell. You draw a man, you don't have to draw his insides! Don't you know I worry about you?"

Siew Lai had taken to wearing her hair in a smart chignon, held by two jade hairpins handed down from a great grandmother said to have married an important magistrate in Canton, a fact she never failed to impress upon new acquaintances. "My family, ah, on my father's side is very rich. My great grandfather had many bond-maids, ah!" She would raise her loud voice so that all could hear her. Her loudness irritated him, more so now than ever before. His feelings for her had changed. If only she could shut her big mouth, he thought, and simply lie on the bed letting him do what he liked with her. In the dark, her body was soft and yielding, with a life of its own, a separate entity to which his animal maleness could respond.

"Now I'm here, when will you see me, ah?" The question was softly asked with eyes coyly lowered, a gesture calculated to soothe his ire.

"You're here, I'll see you. No need to say when! Not leaving tomorrow, are you?"

"No, no." She sighed. "I found a woman's letter in Ah Kiong's pocket."

"You search his pockets regularly?" he sounded surprised.

"If I don't, how would I know what he's doing? One woman after another, he's the death of me, I tell you! No interest in the shop! I do everything! He just stretches out his hand!"

"You like that, don't you? You want to control him," he smiled, raising an eyebrow quizzically so that she could not tell whether he was laughing at her or was just amused.

"You men, ah, all alike! Laugh at me, laugh! Lucky I read the letter. The woman is big with his child! And young too!"

"So?"

"So I know what the fool has done behind my back! I turn a blind eye as long as he doesn't let a woman cling to him, with claims on my shop! Now he's got a bit of money, he wants a concubine. I told him, ah, his young chick is out to get his money, I warned him. Don't come back to me when she's taken all your money, I said. Who'll look after you when you're broken like a spent horse? Not me, ah! I told him straight. Don't come crawling back after you've been squeezed dry, I said. I won't give you a cent!"

She wiped her face with the white handkerchief again. But the hard glint in her eyes remained like that of a veteran's in the war of wills in which tenderness had no place.

"You'll stop giving him his money?" he asked.

"Ha! I stopped already! What I say I do, ah! You don't agree?"

"I didn't say that," he muttered. "You always do what your heart wants."

He was getting tired of being drawn into another lengthy discussion of her marital woes again.

"Hmmm, Ah Loong, why so cold to me?" she asked softly. "You know what my heart wants?" She was whispering once again and lowered her eyes as before. "I saw Dr Tan this morning. For months, ah, I've had a pain in my left side. Here, ah," she patted the top of one large breast. "And here under the shoulder blades. Ah, here, at the neck too."

In a stage whisper, she gave him to know that she had been thoroughly examined by Dr Tan, and went into details where the old man had touched and probed her, her voice growing louder as she described how the old doctor's fingers had poked inside here and stroked lightly there, affectedly waving her hands in front of her face, lamenting the vulgarity of the medical profession, especially those who looked after women's ailments, she complained. Her back still ached, she sighed, and if it weren't for the worry of collecting certain gambling debts owing to her by various persons in Singapore, she would never have travelled all the way down here to suffer and ache like this at night, and he not caring at all.

"Enough! Stop your talk, ah, woman," he said. "I've no money to pay you yet! I'll see you tonight. Your room, eight o'clock."

He rose from the bench and left his supper unfinished.

19

Yoke-lin was waiting for Master Loong in the deserted hall of the Temple of the Eight Immortals. She was pacing up and down between the rows of ancestral tablets and wishing she had not agreed to come. But Yee Soh had arranged everything. Master Loong's magical powers were respected throughout the cabaret world, and many women had gone to him for help to gain the hearts of the men they 'loved'. Here was hope that she would regain Kim San and defeat the vixen who had stolen his heart. Magic must be fought with magic and charms with charms, Yee Soh had advised, and Yoke-lin did not need much to persuade her that nothing was unscrupulous in the battle for a man's heart.

The impassive faces of the gods, towering statues of gilt and wood, gave no sign of any forthcoming help in the flickering gloom of the altar lamps. And yet, Yoke-lin's hopes had been stirred by the success stories she had heard. No gods had ever descended to help ordinary mortals; yet myths and legends persist in fanning beliefs in the heavenly powers, for life without hope, or even its illusion, would be utterly unbearable. Dreams however shallow, hopes however faint, desires however secret and unfulfilled at least give us a reason to live, if not to die.

Yoke-lin was no different. Tentative in her hopes and fearing disappointment, yet desirous of anything that could help, she was willing to believe one minute, clouded with doubts the next. However, she reminded herself that she had nothing to lose. It was a cure that might or might not work.

The sudden sharp notes plucked from the strings of a pipa sliced through her thoughts. The sharp quavers and semi-quavers pierced her heart like a flight of arrows as the tumultuous notes rose and fell in succession with the sudden twists and turns of a harp in discord. Then the conflict stopped as suddenly as it had begun. And a lilting melody, light and sweet, came floating down the hall, teasing and wooing the listener. Note after note, clear and singular, dripped from the eaves like raindrops in the aftermath of a storm, flowing into puddles, congregating in pools, merging into a mellifluous stream of sounds. Eddying like a leitmotif of her troubled heart, the rising cadenza took a sudden plunge, leaving an unfathomable silence in the vast emptiness of the temple hall. Straining to catch that one last note which would tell the listener the depth into which it had plunged, Yoke-lin stood entranced by the moongate. There was a long pause. Then a clear note plucked from a single pipa string dropped into the dark waters and rippled through her heart. She was mesmerised.

Master Loong put down his pipa and came towards her, raising his clasped hands in a silent salute. She bowed as she would to a Buddhist monk in saffron robes, and as if amused by her mark of respect, he grinned and quickened his steps. His boyish grin lit up the quiet intensity of his eyes which seemed to acknowledge her presence and probed the inner recesses of her mind.

"I, er, I'm Yee Soh's friend," she hesitated, "Pang Yoke-lin."

"Come in! My apologies for keeping you waiting, Madam Pang. Please excuse me, I'll order tea."

The way he raised his arms and bowed, and the way his Cantonese rolled out from deep down his throat reminded her of the powerful medium of the Ninth Lord of the Heavens. His sitting room was dominated by large scrolls of the Eight Immortals. She stood in front of the painting of the Immortal Beggar Monk done in broad black strokes and jagged lines highlighting the monk's craggy forehead, deep-set eyes and the pair of bony hands holding a gourd believed to contain the secret of his miracle cures. She moved to the next painting, that of the Celestial Scholar executed in smooth flowing strokes depicting a serene face full of compassion in counterpoint to the ferocious tiger crouched at his feet.

"Faces are not what they seem, Madam Pang."

She turned and came face to face with a pair of dark piercing eyes, penetrating her reserve, and in their reflection, she caught a glimpse of a small woman, herself, anxiously gazing into eyes which seemed to belong to a being from another world. Alarmed, she shook her head and broke the momentary spell.

Master Loong bowed and turned away, carrying a tray of porcelain cups to the table. He motioned her to sit down. An old woman entered with a pot of tea. He dismissed her with a wave of his hand.

"She's dumb. Poisoned by her husband's second wife." His tone was as casual as one remarking upon the fine weather.

She watched him pour a little hot tea into each cup, swirl the tea in it and fling it contents away in the traditional peasant manner of cleaning a teacup. He did not seem in a hurry to serve her, enfolding each small cup in the palm of his broad hand, stroking its smooth rim, letting her wait until satisfied that he was the master, he grasped the teapot firmly in his right hand and poured out the tea. Then he held his cup aloft in a silent toast to the spirits of the night and tossed off his tea in one gulp like a man quaffing a cup of wine. He seemed pleased that Yoke-lin was intrigued by his bit of play-acting.

"Now tell me, Madam Pang, what can I do for you?" he asked.

She was intensely aware of his eyes fixed upon her face as she answered him, knowing that he knew all along the kind of help she required.

"I've seen you before," she said.

"You may have," he replied calmly. "I go to many temples here and in Malaysia."

"Do you visit Anson? Temple of the Ninth Lord?"

"Ah, I go there once a year."

"Then I've met you before!" she exclaimed, pleased that he was not a total stranger. "You helped my relative. She, er, she got a son."

"Aaah, many women who come to me have been helped," he chuckled, the mischievous twinkle in his eye inviting her to share his pleasure, and she had to smile.

"Give me the date and time of your birth," he said.

She handed him the piece of paper on which she had scribbled the information. He grasped her hand and held it firmly in his own, spreading out her fingers. He examined the lines on her palm, tracing their intricate pattern with his forefinger, moving slowly across her hand which lay helplessly in his, its secrets open to his scrutiny.

"To tell the truth, Madam Pang," he released her at last, "your case is not easy. You're carrying too many burdens from your past lives. Let me examine the moles on your back. Follow me please." He stood up and waited for her.

She got up as in a dream and followed him into a small cubicle, partitioned off from the sitting room by a thick curtain. Inside was a bare wooden bed. He motioned her to unbutton her blouse. She obeyed, baring her fair shoulders and part of her back, painfully conscious all the while of his presence behind her.

"Don't worry, Madam Pang. I'm only going to circle the moles on your back with red ink, so I can read their message clearly."

His deep voice was kind and reassuring. His frankness shamed her that she should have allowed even a wisp of doubt to taint the purity of his intentions, and so, quickly, she pulled her blouse down a little lower in an unconscious gesture of remorse and conciliation. He stirred the ink. She braced herself for the first stroke of his vermillion brush. As its gentle tip touched her lightly on the nape of her neck, a pleasant quivering ran down her spine. A cool wet circle was being drawn on her back, but so careful was he not to touch her unnecessarily that every stroke of his brush upon her flesh was slow and deliberate, moving back and forth, back and forth rhythmically, cool sable upon warm flesh, stroke by stroke, soothing away the rigidity of her back, and as the minutes passed, slowly changing it into yielding flesh, rising and falling with the rhythm of her breathing that matched the rhythm of his brush strokes, lulling her till she had to bite her lips to fight off the tiny shivers of pleasure, rippling through her body.

"Madam Pang, I've finished. Please dress."

His whisper, close to her ear, made her flush with shame like one caught in a compromising position. She dressed hurriedly and followed him out of the room.

"I will consult the gods and let you know," he was saying as he ushered her through the gate.

"When?" she mumbled.

"Come next week," he bowed and the gate was shut.

"He likes you, ah!" Yee Soh gushed as soon as Yoke-lin had related the incident to her. "He never sees people out. That dumb woman usually does it."

"Aiya, Yee Soh, what nonsense you speak!"

Yoke-lin was impatient with the older woman's enthusiasm. But secretly, she was more annoyed with herself that she had not been repulsed by the medium's attention.

"This means he'll work the charm for you. Not easy, ah! Got to fast for many days, they say. Then you'll have to go to his temple in Ping Shan. Even some minister's wife went there, I heard."

"How long must I stay there?"

"Don't know. Maybe a few days."

"Then what about Kim San?" Yoke-lin asked, a little worried.

"What about him? He's charmed by the vixen; you think he cares? He'll be happier if you're not here to disturb him! Just tell him you're going to Malaysia to visit relatives, mah."

A week later, Master Loong sent a message through Yee Soh that Yoke-lin should visit him at his mountain abode.

"Yoke-lin, ah, don't worry now. Do as he says. He'll help you. Many barren women have gone to him for the cure and come back with child," Yee Soh nodded knowingly. "Trust me, I won't tell anyone."

20

Lightning flashed across the sky and dark grey clouds loomed above the summit of Ping Shan as the little red bus, with its load of women, all devotees of Master Loong, turned off the trunk road and plunged down a dirt track through the bush and lallang. The red bus struggled up the narrow mountain road, the sky above ominous with the signs of an impending tropical storm. Lightning flashed again and again as Yoke-lin gazed up fearfully at the shrouded summit of Ping Shan, the abode of the Eight Immortals.

Ping Shan was part of the Malaysian Main Range, she was told, that stretched all the way up north as far as China, and was the route taken by the monks of Shaolin when they fled from the scourge of the Chings. With them came the magic and martial arts of the famed Shaolin Temple. The local people believed that the ancient monks, who could tame the wind and raise terrible storms with the help of demons, still lived in these craggy limestone hills. Their white cliffs stood stark against the darkened skies when the sumatras raced across the seas with winds and rains that lashed the padi and flooded the fields.

A sharp clap of thunder cracked the cool crisp air. The skies broke. The sudden torrential downpour drowned the roar of the little bus clinging to the side of the mountain. The windscreen wipers swished to and fro in vain for the screen remained covered with a blanket of water. The bus driver switched on the headlamps, peering cautiously through the storm. "In all my years of driving up this road, ah, I've never seen such a storm," he muttered. "Nam-moh-or-li-toh! Save us Buddha!"

Water poured down the mountainside, rolling over

the bare outcrops, gushing out of porous rocks, dripping from the sodden trees onto the dense undergrowth, and swelling the hillside streams into raging rivers that filled the air with the sound of rushing waters like a horde of invisible spirits.

Yoke-lin and her fellow passengers clung to their seats as their bus jerked forward, stopped, and jerked again. Many of them were sick. The other side of the narrow road dropped sheer to a deep and heavily wooded ravine where creepers and tall grasses covered the trees, forming shadows of unfathomable depths. Yoke-lin turned away lest the evil spirits beckoned her and the bus toppled over. "Say your prayers!" Mrs Choy, the group leader, shouted above the storm. "Fling a red packet out of the window! Give the spirits an ang pow!"

Yoke-lin pulled her jacket tighter round her shoulders. The air was cold with a heavy mist. Their bus coughed and strained up the hill road, hugging the bends, and with each jerk, a passenger was sick. But Yoke-lin held on, determined not to let go. Not this time. She had come so far. Kim San was hers. He belonged to her, her last chance to secure a man she need never share with another woman. He was divorced. Free to marry again. If not for the vixen, he would have married her and bought her a house. The more she thought of it, the more she was sure of it. That vixen must have cast a spell over her man, and it was her duty now to free him and protect him from falling prey to such marauders. It was her maternal duty, too, to secure a nest for Yenti and see her daughter through the years of education ahead.

Jerking in tandem with the little red bus, she soon came to the comforting conclusion that this trip up the mountain was not for herself alone. It was her duty and responsibility as would-be wife and mother to seek protection for her family and free its members from bewitchment. This was what any good woman would do. That she had found her previous visits to the medium of the Eight Immortals pleasurable and the presence of Master Loong intriguing, did not surface in her mind as well-defined as a thought, not even as fleeting as a feeling, but all the same, without being unconscious of it, she was wrapped in sweet trepidation for what was to come. What it was, she had not the faintest idea, and because she did not know, all the more the unknown of Ping Shan beckoned her.

The storm almost drowned out the words of Charlie Wong as he paced restlessly up and down the back room of Ping Shan Temple.

"This has to stop, you hear me? And Ah Loong, you see to it!" he thundered.

But as Ah Loong continued to scrape the dirt from under his finger nails, indifferent to his uproar, Charlie was incensed.

"You asleep, ah? This new headman is stirring up a pot of trouble! The villagers always pay! Now they say no. What does this mean, ha? You tell me!"

Charlie was furious. His reputation as big boss was at stake and so was that of the White Crane's. The villagers had dared to refuse to pay for a fund to finance the local big shot's re-election. A lot more could be at stake if this defiance spread to other villages.

"Ah Loong, you've been away in Singapore too long! Don't leave this time! I will tell you when to go!"

Master Loong looked up at last. The White Crane would blame him for its waning influence sooner or later, but Charlie needed to be reminded of the promise he had made last year.

"You forget, Charlie Wong, I've finished. No more of this. You promised me last year."

"Last year was last year, this year is this year! Listen,

if that son of a whore goes to the police, you and this temple are finished! Finished!"

Charlie Wong spat at him and missed, his gob of spit trickling down the wall. Master Loong moved away. He stood by the window, gazing out at the sodden shacks and the wind-lashed trees while behind him, Charlie Wong continued to fume and fret. But he was too seasoned a dog to care now.

"You listen to me, you!" Charlie shouted at him. "Big Tree Log has found a way into that son of a dog's house. He does his part, you do yours, hear me?"

The medium remained silent. Charlie went out, slamming the door in frustration. It was but a small victory. Still its sweetness was like a cool draught down a thirsty throat.

Master Loong lay on the bed, sighed, and closed his eyes. The storm outside continued unabated. Was there no escape from the White Crane? It hovered and swooped down upon those who tried to flee from its shadow. He was getting on in years, he thought, and should stop such work. Be a simple caretaker in this temple, not a fraud and a quack. If only the powers that be would let him! Something in the clean crisp air of the mountain always gnawed at his heart whenever he returned. He should never have returned. The spirit of the old monk haunted the temple; it was in the room where he meditated, the trees he had planted and the rocks he had painstakingly arranged and chiselled. But look, old man, look! Hadn't he tried? He was staring at the stump on his left hand, a brute reminder of the time when he had tried to run away and the White Crane Boss had sent his warriors to cut off his index finger. They had pressed him down, three of them, while the fourth chopped it off, and he had fainted. But that was years ago when his anger and passion to do the honourable thing had not yet dissipated in the steamy massage parlours, lurid bars and crowded gambling dens where he sank deeper and deeper into the mire, accumulating debts and more debts, failing through various causes, mostly his own mistakes and weaknesses - aiya, he should have listened to the old man - till piled high with regrets, they bound him the tighter each time he tried to flee from his addictions.

"Too late, too late," his old man had cried just before he died, the tears rolling down his eyes. And that was another lesson he still had not learnt: that by the time a man realized the goodness or evil of anything, it was always too late.

Groaning, Master Loong pulled himself up with an effort, and stood looking out at the rain behind the window's iron grills, an aged tiger sniffing the air of the jungle beyond. He recalled how his mother used to sing to him whenever, as a child, he was stuck at home on rainy days.

"The big rains come flooding down the street,
Younger Brother is at home,
Embroidered slippers warming his feet.
Elder Brother is struggling home,
His back loaded with rice and meat."

Too late, too late! He shook his head and turned away from the window. He dabbed away a tear of self-pity. Charlie Wong was right. He was too indebted to the White Crane which had provided for all his needs these many years. What more could he ask for? What could he do outside of this life? In the temples, amidst the gods, he was somebody. He himself did not know how some of these women were cured; how those complaining of aches and pains could walk again when touched by him; the barren ones bore children, and some regained spouses who had strayed into others' arms.

Years of an unconscious habit, of refusal to pursue a thought to its logical end, had protected him, and he believed that without much effort on his part, willy-nilly, perhaps the gods did really work through him. Who could tell for sure? He was a descendant of monks, he soothed himself, and after so many years of seances, how would he know when the gods came and when they left. He was only their instrument. They and the White Crane had given him a relatively easy life. Should he, at his age now, exchange a life of wearing embroidered slippers for a life of carting empty barrels in the rain?

He was not a man given to long periods of reflection. His was a life among thousands of unexamined lives. Life was to be lived as it was handed to him, shaped by events governed by fate, determined by the choices he had made in the past and the life he would lead in the next reincarnation. His religious practices had taught him that a man's life was shaped by gods who could be placated and bribed with gifts. Man was but a pawn in Buddha's palm from which even the great Monkey King could not escape. If he had not been born into his set of circumstances with his particular bent of character, he might have been a doctor or a lawyer instead of a medium. But as the saying goes, "Each man a different fate, each tree different roots. A willow will not grow into a pine. All is but fate."

As long as he was not asking his devotees to steal or kill, he was not doing them harm. And if illusion, rituals and magic potions rekindled hope in desperate hearts, then what he was doing was not really deceitful. Did not monks, priests and physicians ministering to the sick and dying, the hurt and grieving, do the same? He did not force people to do anything against their own will. He suggested, they agreed. He displayed and they bought - amulets, charms, potions and rituals. He had a living to make, and if it was fated that he should earn his living in this manner, then so be it.

His heart went back to the old gods and the spirits of the earth, the ancient myths of fox spirits and snake goddesses, the brotherhood of secret societies, the mystery of blood-sacrifices, the lost, intense passions of men, caught in the confluence of the old and new winds of life, with little education to comprehend the contradictions both in themselves and the world around them.

21

Master Loong stood at the top of the temple steps, waiting for the red bus, his face as calm as Ping Shan after a storm. The village below the temple, a cluster of attap houses belonging to the vegetable farmers, was a haven of green and mists on the banks of a stream, now a torrent of rushing water. The patchwork of vegetable plots, gleaming emerald in the rays of the setting sun breaking through the mists, greeted the new arrivals.

The women stamped their feet and blew warm breaths upon their hands, speaking in hushed whispers. Paths of stamped earth ran down the slopes, losing themselves in the lush greenness of the sub-tropical bush of lianas, creepers and ferns. Beyond the bush was the implacable silence of the jungle, a silence broken occasionally by the screech of a monkey.

The women trudged up the narrow track of broken bricks toward the wooded slopes. Nestling in the shadows was the Temple of the Eight Immortals, lit by the faint rose colour that briefly enlivened the slate grey skies. Master Loong hurried down the steps to meet them.

"Ready?" shouted Mrs Choy the next morning. "Those ready, go outside and line up in the courtyard!"

Twenty women went out quietly, their mood as sober as the black robes they had donned for the penitential rites. They were doing penance for the sins of their past lives. Yoke-lin adjusted her sash and joined the file of women in the courtyard. Led by attendants beating drums and gongs, they began their slow agonising walk round the courtyard.

At every third step, a gong sounded. The women knelt and kowtowed, knocking their foreheads on the cold hard stones. Then getting up, they walked another three steps and knelt again at the sound of the gong, and kowtowed to atone for the sins of the past, stretching back into time immemorial. She could have been a child murderer in another life, Yoke-lin thought, and prayed for forgiveness from the gods.

They returned to the temple and sat on the floor facing the Master who sat cross-legged on a raised dais. As he chanted, they followed him, voices throbbing with the fervour of belief. His richly tanned face spoke to her of the sun, the wind and the rain. His starched white robe, ironed till it shone, enveloped him like a protective barrier as he calmly looked past them, attentive to the words of his gods.

"Or-me-toh-fu! Or-me-toh-fu!"

Another being from another world in communion with realms beyond, his face was distinguished by the greying hairs at his temple, and as they chanted, it seemed to glow with the wisdom of the ancient masters. Yoke-lin bowed her head. The discordant chimes of the gongs bounced off the walls, stirring distant echoes in her heart. She stared at his face a long time, hoping that he would look in her direction, but his eyes were closed.

"Or-me-toh-fu, or-me-toh-fu!"

Then he stopped. The women looked up. He turned his head, looked in her direction and gave her a brief smile. She knelt and kowtowed to the Immortal Scholar smiling down on her.

Later that morning, she was asked to see him in his study. He stood up when she entered, and strode towards her with arms outstretched in a gesture of welcome. Then just as he reached her at the doorway, he put his hands abruptly behind him.

"Ah, Madam Pang, I bid you welcome at Ping Shan,"

he spoke formally. "Long have I waited to talk with you. Yours is a complicated case. Many things to consider and discuss, for the ritual is a very lengthy one."

His formal Cantonese sounded classical to her uneducated ears, and she was awed by this evidence of his learning.

"Come, I'll present you to the gods," he said. He was walking beside her and she kept her eyes on his feet. Such big broad feet used to walking long distances. "Indeed, Madam Pang, up here in this air, I can walk for miles." It was uncanny the way he had caught her fleeting thought.

His private meditation room was lined with the scrolls of the Eight Immortals. On the small altar, a wisp of smoke was curling out of an incense urn. She clasped her hands and bowed to the Immortals. He leant back into his large comfortable armchair while she sat on the edge of hers. In his hand, he was slowly counting a string of worry beads. One by one with a soft click, they slipped through his fingers; he was in no hurry although there were other devotees waiting to see him.

"Master Loong, will the gods help me?" she asked. She knew she must have sounded impatient.

"Yes, Madam Pang, with the right rituals, the gods will help those who believe," he replied, looking straight into her eyes.

She bowed her head, a little angry with herself that she should feel so awkward in his presence. He waited for her to speak again. But she had nothing to say. No words came.

At last, he asked her, very quietly, "Tell me, is there another woman in his life?"

She nodded, and there was another pause.

"For how long?" he asked.

"Almost a year," she muttered.

There was another pause before he finally asked, "When did he last come to you as man to his wife?"

She did not answer him. She was miserable and wretched. How could she tell him that Kim San had not so much as touched her these many many months? Hurt, long buried under layers of anger and righteousness at his betrayal, forced tears into her eyes. She looked away. "I want a son," she said and bit her lips.

Master Loong bent down to light another stick of incense. A tiny flame shot up as he lit a match. The stick lit and smouldered with a thin thread of smoke winding up to the ceiling, a silent plea to the gods.

"Madam Pang," he looked up, his eyes piercing into her soul, "not an easy task, not easy." He shook his head slowly. "You must understand, it's not up to me. The gods decide, and the burdens of the past must be washed away." He paused and seemed to be considering and weighing the factors while the soft click-click of his worry beads filled the small room.

He was her only hope now, and while the cosy small room seemed safe, the vastness beyond Ping Shan and the years rolling before her were fraught with unnameable fears.

"What...er...what must I do?" She was almost whispering in her reluctance to break the quiet intimacy enveloping them in a way she could not grasp.

"Aaaah, Madam Pang, the gods have many ways," he smiled. "There's the Lotus Ritual, very difficult, handed down through the masters." He sighed, "But it takes too much, far too much out of me."

She squirmed under the portrait of the Immortal Monk with the unrelenting stare, fearful that he might now refuse to help her.

"Don't worry, Madam Pang," he said, "I cannot refuse to help you. I cannot disobey the gods. They sent you here to me, and I will do as they decree."

And she was startled once again by his response to her unspoken thought.

"I must do what I must," he was muttering, "and you must do what you must."

"But what must I do?" she asked.

"Aaah, in the Lotus Ritual, meditate and pray, fast for many days and, and there'll be a ritual bath. But not here, not here," he said, following her gaze towards the crowd congregating outside. "I've a hut in the hills, just behind the temple. There, I'll prepare you for the gods."

"For the gods?" she asked.

"For the gods," he answered, looking into her eyes and smiling like an old friend sharing a secret.

That night a crowd of excited villagers arrived, carrying torches, gongs and drums, waiting to escort Master Loong to the new headman's house. It was bedevilled by spirits hurling pots and pans out of the windows, they reported. Pots and pans flying out of nowhere! The work of mischievous spirits! The children were frightened and the crops might fail! Everyone had a story to tell that night.

"Wah! Powerful spirits, ah! Never seen the likes before! Not since the old monk cleansed Ping Shan years ago. Before that, ah, our vegetables died! Now they grow," the old Hakka farmer spoke to Yoke-lin in his thick dialect.

The swift dark night descended upon them. The villagers lit their torches and hurricane lamps.

"Once in Telok Bunga, ah, Master Loong saved a man," Mrs Choy recounted. "The man was driving to Ipoh. Midnight, aiya, you know that trunk road, so dark, no street lamps. A Malay woman stopped his car. Very beautiful, invited him home. The greedy man followed. The next morning, ah, he found himself in the graveyard, a dead frog in his mouth. He was so sick, ah, the doctors thought he'd die! Then his wife came to Master Loong."

Mrs Choy helped the Master with his ceremonial robes and gave his red cape a final tug.

"Follow me," he told his devotees. "Pray and keep close together. Chant with me, weaken the spirits."

Bands of men beating gongs and drums marched behind him. Yoke-lin and the women followed. Their saffron-robed Master was leading the vanguard like the powerful Abbot in the storming of Madam White Snake's pagoda, a majestic figure wearing a red and yellow cape billowing in the night breeze.

The procession stopped outside the headman's house. Two large dishes flew out of the dark windows and crashed at the Master's feet. The crowd fell back with a gasp! But Master Loong calmly kicked the pieces aside and stood his ground.

The drums fell silent as he raised a bright blue urn slowly above his head. Suddenly, he leapt into the air, his red cape bristling like the feathers of a fighting cock. The drums burst into a pulsating beat. He pranced, shadow-boxing invisible enemies as the gongs clanged and the cymbals clashed!

"Nam-mo-or-li-toh-fu! Nam-mo-or-li-toh-fu!" the crowd was chanting, led by the Master's booming voice rising above the beat of the drums. They circled the headman's blighted house and stopped in front of the main door.

Master Loong raised an imperious arm. The crowd stopped their chant. The villagers' torchlights flashed upon the silent house. The Master turned to face the front door, legs apart, knees bent as in a kung-fu stance. Aik! He leapt into the air, kicked open the door and rushed inside, holding the urn in front of him like a shield. A piercing scream rang out! Startled night birds flew out of the bushes. The young children cried and clung to their mothers. Every torch was aimed at the doorway. After what seemed like a very long time, Master Loong emerged smiling, the urn held high above his head.

The villagers cheered! The drums rolled a long tattoo.

The children pranced up and down, in time to their beat, imitating the lion dancers on New Year's Day. Yoke-lin breathed a sigh of relief and followed the procession back to the temple.

In the courtyard, the exulted villagers built a pyre and threw sticks of incense into the flames. The temple attendants flung in stacks of joss papers and the flames rose even higher. Master Loong threw the urn into the fire. A loud explosion brought the men hurrying in with buckets of water from the temple's well. They doused the flames.

"Aiya, look! Blood!" a woman cried out.

A dark liquid was oozing from the urn, seeping into the ground as the flames around it hissed and crackled.

"The demon's blood!" the woman clutched at Yoke-lin's arm to stop herself from trembling.

All the devotees later agreed that that was the moment when they felt an icy breath of wind blowing through the courtyard.

"Nam-mo-or-li-toh-fu!" Master Loong's chanting had an urgency which made all the villagers kneel and kowtow to the "Tamer of Evil" as he was called in those parts.

22

The chimes of the temple bells grew more and more faint the higher they climbed. The limestone rocks were bathed in gold by the setting sun and the magical hour of silence hung between night and day. All the birds had gone to roost.

Yoke-lin followed Master Loong up the winding path, and a deep longing for some meaning and purpose under this vast arch of sky made her heart ache indescribably. How intensely aware she was of that current of energy locked in those limbs striding before her, covered by a thin white shirt. He turned to help her climb over a rock, and the warmth of his hand made her flush.

They stood on a small plateau overlooking the village. A rough stone path led to a tiny hut squatting in the shade of the jungle trees. The breeze was especially cool here, and wisps of mist were weaving in and out of the tall grasses, suggesting unseen beings. Night would soon be upon them, and she felt the presence of spirits watching from behind the trees and rocks. The warmth of his voice was reassuring. "The Earth God will protect you. Just remember what I said."

They entered the hut. He lit a candle and placed it on the red altar.

"When this goes out, don't be afraid. The messenger of the gods will come."

He showed her into the next room which was bare except for a mattress on the raised wooden floor. Stooping down, he untied the bundle he had been carrying, and took out a brown jar.

"Drink this," he said, handing it to her. "The wine of the Immortals will strengthen you."

The wine soothed her nerves and warmed her bones. Night had descended and the air outside was chilly.

"You must stay here alone, but don't be afraid, I'll be out there and I'll come in if you're in any danger. Tonight the lesser spirits might disturb us. We may have to fight them."

He went out closing the door behind him. She could hear him settling down for the night. The room was not as dark as she had feared for streams of light came from the candle in his room through cracks in the thin partition. She sat on the floor, calmed by his presence.

But the night was long, and little by little, the rustling of the leaves in the breeze and the soft scuttling sounds of the night creatures made her uneasy. Let no black rat come near her, she prayed. Nor a spider crawl over her in the dark. The strange cries of the night birds echoed through the hills. She tried to meditate as he had instructed, but the wine was making her drowsy. She tried to keep awake, but her tired eyelids were drooping. No sound came from the next room. A single beam of light was dancing, flickering blue and green in front of her. Could it be the spirit of a lost soul seeking to enter her unsuspecting body? She closed her eyes and prayed.

A bull frog croaked and she opened her eyes. She could not remember how long she had been sitting up before she was aware of the white beast watching her from across the room. Its eyes were burning green and gold, now fierce, then warm and inviting. Nearer, they seemed to say, nearer, come nearer, their magnetic powers drawing her towards the beast of prey. It crept towards her, beckoning. She watched mesmerised but unafraid.

It leapt upon her, and she was thrown upon its back, racing through the night, through the dark foliage bowing like slaves before their master's stride. Seated astride the king of the jungle, gripping him between her thighs, she was riding him, riding him with every thrust of his majestic muscles as wave upon wave they rippled beneath her, carrying her high into the night sky. Through the darkness they flew, deep into the shadows of unfathomable depths. Deeper and deeper they pressed on, harder and harder the Tiger thrust, his eyes gleaming green and gold. She clutched his shoulders, feeling each throb of his muscles as he tore through her heart, mauling her breasts, devouring her. Twisting and turning, she wrestled with him but the fierce beast pressed her down, down, down. Again and again, he pressed against her, breaking her resistance till she lay moaning in sweet defeat.

The grey silence of night gave way to the sounds of dawn, and she found herself lying on the mattress in the corner. Tap, tap, tap, the knocking grew louder and more insistent. With a start, she realised that this was not part of her dream. She got up, pulling her robe around her before opening the door.

"Good morning, Yoke-lin, breakfast is here. I have to leave now."

He was already out of the hut before she could thank him. Clutching her robe, she stood at the doorway, watching his white figure striding down the path with the sinewy grace and power of a jungle beast. The drops of dew gleamed green and gold in the morning sun. As he turned the corner and disappeared from view, wisps of mist wafted away. She leaned against the door-post, feeling the ground slipping beneath her as her limp body recalled the strength and force of the white beast, and that strange confusion of fear, resistance and desire to submit to a power greater than herself. The dream had been so real.

23

The days passed uneventfully. In the evening it was drizzling again and grey mists enveloped Ping Shan. Yoke-lin had grown used to staying in the hut, listening to the rain hitting its zinc roof or sitting outside, watching the tree squirrels scamper among the branches, or pottering in the small vegetable plot, passing the time languidly. The tall trees, silent in the rain, and the thick wet bushes beneath them formed an impenetrable wall behind which lurked the dark beings she had gotten used to. This evening, the simian face of a lone gibbon watched her from among the trees like a spirit of the hills. The shadows were lengthening as the air grew colder. He should be here soon, she thought, as she lit the oil lamp and laid the table for two. Strange that she should feel that she had been doing this all her life. But the languor in the air of these hills had made her mind sluggish, and she did not examine her feeling.

A rustle made her look up in time to see his white figure emerging from the tall grasses nearby. He cocked his head and looked at her roguishly, the light of the setting sun in his eyes.

"Tonight we begin," he said. "The gods have spoken at last."

The gravity of his tone and the intensity in his eyes made her a little uneasy. What if she should fail him, and the Immortals reject her request? There was much to be done for the ritual and a thin thread of excited anticipation wove in and out of the myriad chambers of her heart. Her hands trembled a little as she ladled out the rice, trying to hide the blush on her face.

He sat opposite her and began to eat in the comfortable silence that had crept up upon them like dusk, short and sudden, turning the tropical evening into night. Secretly, she took pleasure in the illusion as she watched him eat. He looked like any of the farmers around here who had just returned home to eat what their wives had cooked for the evening meal. For the time being, his gods were allowing him to be himself.

Master Loong placed the oil lamp on the altar from where it threw shadows upon the walls like dark beings gathering round to listen in on their conversation. Night insects flew round and round the lamp, hurtling themselves against its glass cover.

"So, you still think having a son is good?" he asked her.

She nodded and ate her rice slowly, listening as usual to his often inconsequential and unrelated talk.

"It's true," he said, "that a man seldom forgets the mother of his sons - unless he forgets his ancestors. When he grows old, he will think about the son who will lead his funeral procession."

"I want a son so I can have a family and a home. Every bird has its nest," she said.

"How true, how very true!"

They ate as they talked within the circle of lamplight and she felt safe with him while the shadows and the muted noises of the jungle surrounded them.

"New Year's Eve with no home to return to is the loneliest time for those of us without families," he said with a wry smile that made her feel he was a kindred spirit. "Aiya, many a time, too many times I've gotten drunk! I hear the poet Li Bai used to get drunk too. My cup of wine, my shadow and myself! Aaah, what harmony!"

"I'm not learned like you," she replied. "My mother died when I was very young. I had only three years in school."

"When my mother died, I was very young too." He accepted the cup of tea she had poured for him as if it were her duty to serve him.

"I remember New Year's Eve as a good time. No scolding, no beating, eat what we like, ah! Tai Ku, Tai Shook, Ah Jen and me, we sat down to dinner. Steamed chicken with soya sauce. Every family ate the same thing after praying to their ancestors. And on that day I felt safe."

"Safe?" he asked.

"Yes, safe, because I wanted to be like everyone else. People had families, I had a family. They had mothers, I had a mother too. I've always dreamed of a home of my own. Now, ah, I don't care if Kim San only comes home once a month or once a year. Those who marry sailors also live like widows, mah!"

"True, very true," he agreed.

"If I had a son, Kim San would come home to me, even if it's only once a year. He would take care of me and his son and pray to his ancestors in my home. I think a lot these days, ah, and I know I'm not getting younger. Men, ah, don't care how old, they'll roam, but a woman after thirty must settle down."

She did not raise her head, knowing that he was looking at her intently, and they remained silent, listening to the soft patter of the rain outside while they sipped hot tea. She was embarrassed for having spoken so much. But she found his silence comforting during such times, giving her the space in which to adjust to his rhythm.

And his rhythm was vigorous. After each night's ritual, she was exhausted, lying on the mattress, weak and inert because of her fasting, and yet strangely invigorated and relaxed each morning despite the rigours of the night.

The ritual baths were beginning to have an effect on her as he had predicted. She was beginning to feel that there was some beauty left in her yet. The cabaret years and the men, a blur of faces now, had taken their toll, but there was something left in her still which the fragrance of sandalwood, pomelo leaves and rose water was slowly reviving.

By the light of two red candles, he bathed her each night, fully clothed, united as they were by the spirit of the marriage ceremony she had undergone with the Immortal Scholar, represented according to tradition, by a white cockerel held in the Master's hands. Vibrant red coxcomb, bright male eyes and strong sturdy legs tied with a red silk band, the cockerel had been specially bred for such rituals as the tying of the nuptial knot between a human and a spirit from the nocturnal realm.

The bride of the Immortal Scholar had bowed to the Master, representative of the Spirit, holding the white cockerel whose blood he would drink to absorb its essence so that the child of this spiritual union would be strong and wise.

> "Bow to our Father and Mother of Earth,
> One kowtow, two kowtow, three kowtow;
> Bow to the Heavens three times now,
> May Earth, Sky and Man be our witnesses!
> One combing of your hair for longevity,
> White and long may it grow!
> Two combings of your hair for health,
> Tough and strong be the fruit of your womb!
> And now this red band binds you to the trials
> And tribulations of your lives!"

And so each night, he bathed her, pouring essence of rose and rubbing her with holy oil. Then they sat cross-legged on the wooden floor, face to face, two white figures chanting prayers by the candle light.

Breathe deeply and slowly, he said. Relax. Think of the Immortal Scholar and what you would like from him, he whispered, looking more and more like the Immortal himself, and so gentle was he in speech and movement that whenever she was with him, reality seemed unreal and time an eternity. Still and eternal was Ping Shan Hill, the rock of her universe and the still point in her time.

The rich cadence of his chanting and the sonorous tone of his voice was at once comforting, keeping her fears at bay, and discomfiting because he was opening new doors and leading her down strange ways. His presence seemed to grow as they prayed deeper and deeper into the night. And each night she climbed the fabled mountains astride the sinewy trunk of the strange White Beast, soaring into the heavenly skies, leaping from cloud to cloud, seeding. Aaah, let it rain, let it rain! The upsurge of feelings made her ache. Any minute her tendons would break and her heart burst asunder! Harder and harder, she strove to press against the source of life. Harder! Harder! If only her fragile frame would break and disintegrate in one supreme moment when no barriers would be between them, complete and whole in the perfect union of the dance between the phoenix and the dragon!

But the sky at times was an impenetrable mass, hemming her in with the unmoving trees, an inscrutable presence behind an unbending will, still as a praying mantis ready to pounce on its prey. Her limbs grew stiff. The dark forces were tightening their grip on her, she could hardly breathe. A sudden gust blew out the candles, plunging them into dark sunless seas. She was falling as in a dream, deeper and deeper, screaming but no words came. She struggled to reach the surface, flailing her arms in vain. She was floundering in ether, and sinking slowly, slowly. Cool waters washed over her, a whispering presence stroked her, warm and palpable, murmuring words of sweetness, caressing, tracing her curves, weaving in and out, entwining itself about her waist, searching out her secrets, teasing and wooing her out of her hard encrusted self. With sigh after sigh, pushing breasts upwards, opening out like a young flower, she yielded her body like soft clay in the potter's hands, moulding her to receive the stream of life. "Grasp me. Harder. Harder. Squeeze out my essence." The voice was strong and the hands were firm. Harder and harder she pressed. Her heart would break! O, it would break! But he grasped her and hugging her close, carried her through the clouds and rain, and she fell into a deep, deep sleep.

24

She woke up the next morning, alone as usual. Beside the breakfast tray was a small rolled-up scroll. Next to it, on a white sheet of paper were four Chinese characters: Time To Descend Mountain. She had been expecting this moment although she had not expected the days to pass so quickly. Her time was up. She would have to leave Ping Shan and return home to the clamorous world.

But still she lingered. For the moment, she was in no hurry. This hut had been her home. She unrolled the scroll, reading and re-reading the four lines written in his neat calligraphy.

"They have parted,
Their faces and voices separate.
Many are the roads from Ping Shan,
How sad each has to travel alone."

Slowly, she rolled up the scroll and walked out of the hut. It must be her karma that each of them would leave her a poem. She looked back at the flimsy wooden structure made of crudely-sawn planks nailed together. A temporary shelter in a transient world. Those beautiful lines merely signified that they owed each other nothing. Their sojourn was over, and each was free to move on. But if she had been prepared for this moment, she sighed, why was she feeling empty now?

Yenti's Journal

This phenomenon of a romantic bond between "the man of god" and a woman of earth is universal. In the West, the influence of the monk, Rasputin, over the last Tsarina of Russia and other noble ladies, is well-known. Then there is the equally well-known tragic romance between Abelard, the priestly tutor, and his young charge, Heloise, the niece of the bishop. In every city or village parish, there are feminine souls suffering in secret the anguish and agony of the unattainable, and they turn to the man of religion for help.

To whom do these women turn if they do not belong to the church? In this city of many religions and hi-tech sophistication, Chinese cult mediums thrive and make a good living out of the hearts and pockets of the lonely, the depressed, the jilted and the suicidal.

There are frequent reports in the papers of women being molested or seduced by a medium, and I wonder why in the world they consulted him in the first place. What makes them turn to such men? Are they simply illiterate, semi-illiterate, gullible, superstitious and highly susceptible to suggestion? How else can one explain the behaviour of these women, who allow mediums to strip them, presumably to examine their breasts for cancer and their lower parts for diabetes, and to roll eggs over their breasts or rub sweet oils on their bodies? All in the name of the gods, deities and herbal cures.

I have noticed, too, that female devotees outnumber males in any medium cult, and the medium is almost always a man. It does seem to indicate something about women, especially Chinese women that within the foggy realm of cult beliefs and faith healing, there lies probably an acceptable source of sexual pleasure and release for apparently respectable housewives.

Still, that does not quite explain Mother's experience if what I've reconstructed is true. Ping Shan intrigues me and it is not easy to come to terms with the infidelities of one's parents. My step-father has had many women, why can't I accept the fact that Mother has had more than one man? Two, three, four, five, ten, I don't know. After all, she had been a cabaret girl for many years. Was she celibate before she met Ah Pa? That was what she made herself out to be, implying her purity in the midst of cabaret filth. It is this streak of righteousness bordering on dishonesty which I cannot stand!

Mother, if only I had the Cantonese words to confront you! To say what I want to say in your language without sounding crude and coarse.

Living the truth is better than living a lie. That much I've learnt from my convent education. But I know what you would say. You would say: "Parents are the sky and children the earth. Even if you've slept under my bed only once, you're still my child. What parents do with their lives is not for the child to judge! Have I let you go hungry, without clothes or education? Ha! Don't I know that water flows downstream, never up? I don't expect you to repay me. Enough that you can now talk so cleverly to me! Enough that you can earn your own living and not be like me, forever dependent on a man! You look down on me, your own mother!" You would sob and I would be wretched.

That's why I write. I can't talk to you. I can never repay all that you've done for me. Never! I recognise my eternal debt. You carried me nine months in your womb - these are your words - and you did not abort or abandon me.

But Mother, please think again. Did you go to Ping Shan for my sake alone? Did you live your life simply for me? How do you expect me to carry that kind of burden? Mine the guilt for your unfaithfulness! Wasn t your infidelity more an act of vengeance, a repayment in kind for Uncle Ong s infidelity to you? Typical Cantonese vengeance! Ah Pa couldn t protest. As you would say, his mouth was stuffed with a dead cat! You knew his need for capital and the peculiar provision in his First Mother s will. You gave him the son to qualify for that quarter million dollars. Ah Pa might have had his doubts, but he was wise and kept them to himself. So there! You scheming woman, you got him where you wanted, and he married you. The miraculous thing about Ping Shan was that you succeeded in conceiving a boy when it could just as easily have been a girl.

Like mother like daughter. I m beginning to sound as self-righteous as you. After all, is truth all that necessary? Will knowing the truth about Soo Beng s birth be of any use to me, Ah Pa or Soo Beng himself? Will it increase the sum total of our happiness? Let sleeping dogs lie, I seem to hear you say. So be it.

Perhaps Mother was caught off-guard and could not understand the mystery of the passion - the mysterium tremendum , as the Latin scholars had called it - that gripped her, so that upon reflection, she was convinced of her magical union with the gods. Or am I making excuses for her now? The pantheon of gods were her tools for coping with life and its many pitfalls. I doubt whether Cantonese - or any language, for that matter - contains the words to describe her sexual experience on Ping Shan.

And in the long lapse of time between the moment when I first *knew* and the moment when I first *understood*, much water had flowed under the bridge. When I was young, I had judged the world like the young - from the self-righteousness of my ignorance. I had kept my knowledge of Ping Shan from Mother and everyone else, clutching the piece of shame and deceit close to my heart. But now that I have tasted passion myself and felt the sting of its victory, I no longer suffer from the kind of self-righteous ignorance which some people prefer to call innocence. No, I am no longer an innocent girl. And what Mother did or did not do on Ping Shan no longer carries for me the same immense moral dimensions and implications it once did.

Family Mansion

"A mansion with marble lions at the gate,
And three generations under one roof.
Aaah, that is Happiness, Prosperity and Longevity."

Old Immigrant

25

The dark houses in Orchid Garden slept in peaceful oblivion of the loneliness of the woman staring at them from her upstairs window. The two-storeyed terrace houses with little gardens and a car parked on each driveway, and husbands and children inside, looked much like what she had. So what more could a woman like her want, Yoke-lin asked herself.

She had lost some of her slenderness since the birth of Soo Beng three years ago. The thickness around her waist and hips had made it impossible for her to wear the tight-fitting cheongsam of her youth. Her hair, which had been permed fashionably short, framed a tired face.

Kim San was out entertaining clients again. Everybody said that Kim San had prospered because of the birth of her boy, and consequently he had bought this house and car in her name and had even given her a jade bracelet on New Year's Day ... and yet, she sighed an inward sigh, the hollow feeling in her heart had remained. Weary of her perpetual sense of dissatisfaction, she had concluded that the fault was in herself and her fate. She had always thought that a house, a family and a husband would be enough. And Kim San had provided all these and more - he had accepted Yenti into the family too.

Though Yoke-lin could not put it into words, her unhappiness was, and is, essentially the woman's condition. According to the women of old, it is the woman's fate to suffer pain. Pain on leaving home when she marries into another household, pain on her wedding night, pain when her husband sets eyes on another woman, and pain each time a child is born to her. She is cut in two the day she enjoys her first love. The man remains the same. He spends a night with a woman and goes away. His life and body do not change. The woman feels the difference. It is she who conceives and carries the fruit of the night, nine long months in her body. Motherhood changes a woman; fatherhood need not change a man. He brings home the rice and feels he has the right to come and go.

It was now long past midnight. Orchid Garden was deserted except for the buzzing insects around the street lamps. How like those of Ping Shan! They knocked senselessly against the lamps' glass covers, dying by the hundreds in their suicidal frenzy to reach the scorching light. Futile deaths. Why should life struggle to renew itself unless there was hope that the next generation would have a better life than the present? Yenti, she hoped, would be better off than her, just as she herself was better off than her mother.

The clock struck one as she slipped into bed. After a year of playing the devoted father, Kim San had returned to his old ways, and her struggle to acquire a nest had become a struggle to guard her nest.

It was her fate, she sighed, that her men should never spend all their nights with her. She believed that her first meeting with Kim San had been fated. Had she remained in bed instead of going to the Southern despite her cold, she would never have met him. And if Kim San had not made a noise when he tripped over his chair and almost toppled on to her, their eyes would not have caught each other's smiles. He had been a reticent man in need of someone to look after him; she had happened to be there in search of someone to look after. One thing had led to another and gradually, his nights with her became longer and more frequent, his stays lengthening into days, then weeks and months, until finally, Yee Soh raised the rent of her room because there were two lodgers instead of one. Good humouredly, Kim San paid the rent and moved in permanently.

Nothing was said about marriage and family until Soo Beng's arrival. With the birth of a son, Kim San now stood to gain two hundred and fifty thousand dollars when his First Mother died. It was the boy that made Kim San marry her. Not love. She had been naive to think that after the birth of a son, Kim San would be hers completely.

"A chance encounter turning the wheels of fate. You owed him something in your past life; you're repaying the debt now," Master Loong had said. Sometimes she wondered what had become of him. He had not returned to Singapore, not that she would ever see him again. Some said he was in Penang, others that he had gone away to study Balinese magic in the mountains of Indonesia. Who could tell what he might do, the man who said the sky was his roof, the earth his pillow and the moon his wife. She would never be happy following a wanderer.

She started up when she heard Kim San knocking things over in the bathroom. He was drunk again, and wearily, she got up to help him, hoping that the noise would not awaken Yenti and the boy.

Kim San leaned heavily against her as she half-dragged his bulk on to the bed where he sprawled face down. He did not wake up. She lay beside him, unable to close her eyes. Her sleep had fled. His presence disturbed her as much as his absence. His ruddy face in the soft glow of the bedside lamp was that of a chubby boy with a growth of dark fine hair below the bulbous nose. His flabby features were those of Chinese traders who sat all day in their shops, and his paunch the result of too much beer.

Born the son of a concubine whom he called Second Mother, Kim San had not had a happy childhood. There had been too many people in the house, and the women were always squabbling. It was well-known that the patriarch's wife, concubine and mistresses vied and fought with one another for his favours. The old man's sons must have grown up thinking that that was the way to be a man, exercising their male prerogative in sampling mistress after mistress. Yoke-lin often wondered whether it was sibling rivalry that was driving Kim San to build a fortune to match that of his elder brothers, the sons of his father's first wife.

Kim San grunted in his sleep. He turned and pressed against her, exuding stale beer and cigarette smoke. His hand rubbed her breasts mechanically as he lay snoring close to her heart. Her body stiffened instinctively. She twisted and turned this way and that, hoping to avoid what she knew was inevitable. But he tugged at her pants. Her body froze imperceptibly as he rolled on top of her, hard and heavy, and wedged himself between her reluctant thighs. She shut her eyes and braced herself against his poundings.

When it was all over, he rolled on to his side, back towards her, and fell asleep again. Yoke-lin remained lying beside him, staring into the darkness. She did not cry. It was a man's right, she reminded herself. At least he still needed her despite his other women outside. They were still man and wife, united, even if only by this life in the night so divorced from the life of the day, this life that needed no talk and no love. But as far as she knew this was all that mattered to a man, besides having a son and a prosperous business.

The next morning the telephone beside the bed rang. "Hullo!" Kim San growled into it, his head heavy with last night's drinks.

The shrill voice of his eldest sister, Tua Kor, was at the other end. "Come quickly! Our First Mother is dying!" She hung up before he could reply.

26

All eyes turned towards them when Kim San and Yoke-lin entered the living room of the family mansion. None of the old ladies, however, rose to greet them. They were the elders, waiting to be greeted by the younger members of the family. They scrutinised Yoke-lin from head to toe, approving her sombre dress and black court shoes.

"First Aunt, Second Aunt, Third Aunt, Fourth Aunt," Yoke-lin greeted them by their titles.

"Good, you're here. Your mother-in-law is dying, ah," said First Aunt. "Take off that gold chain before you go in."

"Come, come!" A young woman in a floral samfoo suit, a cousin of the family, was beckoning them to follow her. At the doorway she whispered,"Tua Kor is waiting for you. Don't mind those busybodies! They're kaypohs! You wait here, Yoke-lin, sons go in first."

Yoke-lin waited at the doorway, a little awkward, conscious that the old women seated around the rosewood table behind her were talking about her.

"Aiya, the old man has no eyes in heaven, ah! The sons all marry useless wives. The eldest is sick, I hear! He too, ah, plays around like the old tortoise!" one of the aunts said, her face wrinkling up like kneaded dough.

"That one over there, ah, dance hostess last time," Second Aunt sniffed. "The day my son brings home one of those, ha! I'll greet him with a broomstick at the door!"

"Send Tua Pek in the moment he comes!" a strident voice boomed. It was Tua Kor. "The eldest son and he's not here! Ask one of the drivers to go fetch his wife! She's another one! Doesn't know where her own husband is!"

Tua Kor was the eldest daughter of the family who had returned to look after her ailing mother. She was a thin angular woman in her early fifties with hair pulled back into a tight little chignon held by a thick gold pin.

"So many things to do," she grumbled, "and nobody here to do them. I've only got one pair of hands, ah! If I don't do it, nobody'll do it. Come! You must be Kim San's wife! Come with me!"

"No, not yet!" First Aunt called out. "Tua Soh is the first daughter-in-law, she goes in first!"

"She's not here yet!" Tua Kor replied impatiently. "Our mother can't wait for everybody. And she wants to see all her sons and daughters-in-law before she goes. Then she'll close her eyes in peace. If I wait for Tua Soh, it might be too late!"

"Aiya, you younger ones, ah! Do things like this, how can?" Second Aunt protested. "The younger must wait for the elder. Kim San's wife is only number six."

"Aiya, Second Aunt, our mother is dying. I don't want her spirit to plague me next time because I didn't let her see all her daughters-in-law! First to come, first to go in. Tell Tua Soh to come in when she arrives."

Tua Kor pulled Yoke-lin down the corridor, ignoring the protests of the elder aunts.

The matriarch's room was crowded with her sons and daughters, grandchildren, sons-in-law and daughters-in-law, sitting or standing in little groups, silently watching the dying woman's hollow frame gasping for breath. Her eyes were closed, her cheeks sunken and her toothless mouth gaping wide open. Tua Kor pushed Yoke-lin through the crowd till they stood at the matriarch's bedside.

"Our First Mother, can you hear me?" Tua Kor bent over her mother and shouted into her ear. "Kim San and his wife are here! We're waiting for Tua Pek and Tua Soh. Raise your hand if you hear me!"

The rest of the family watched, awed by the rasps of the dying woman as she struggled to raise her hand weighed down by a thick band of translucent jade. It was as if invisible spirits were wrenching the life out of her and she was making one last effort to cling on a few more minutes, fighting hard for breath, unwilling to go till she had seen her eldest son. But her frayed breath, straining in vain, snapped at last. Her mouth dropped in a silent scream before the lips slumped over the toothless gums, a ghastly caricature of death.

"Aiya, aiya, Ah Bu, aaah! First Mother, ah! You all quick! Quickly call mother! Call her! Call your grandma, ah! Don't go yet!" Tua Kor cried. "Don't go! Your eldest son is coming, ah! Aiya, our mother, why didn't you let your eldest son see you before you went?" Tua Kor collapsed on the floor, wailing for her mother who had suffered the misfortune, the ultimate misfortune of dying without receiving the last obeisance of her eldest son. Her unhappy spirit would haunt her descendants and bring them ill-fortune, she cried.

All the women in the room took up Tua Kor's cry. Their wailing voices, rising and falling in rhythmic Hokkien, filled the mansion, weaving a wreath of tears that bonded each member of the family in their public expression of a sorrow which might be unfelt in many private breasts.

But Yoke-lin was touched and had tears in her eyes, for had not the matriarch on her deathbed remembered her and accorded her that gesture of acceptance into the family in calling her to her bedside? She was filled with gratitude, for in that moment she became part of the Ong clan.

27

The next day, a freshly cut bamboo with a white cloth tied at one end was stuck into the ground outside the mansion gate. Above the pair of marble lions guarding the main doorway hung a pair of white lanterns, the sign of mourning. Inside, all pictures and mirrors were covered with red paper for the darkness of death must be warded off by the brightness of red, and all glass must be covered lest it reflect the malevolent spirits hovering near the dead.

The entire Ong clan was gathered at the mansion, for a death in the family is able to bring together members who seldom meet otherwise. For the duration of the wake and the funeral, they came together as fellow mortals reminded of the temporality of life and the finality of death. There was much to do to keep everyone busy and useful - rituals to perform, prayers for the dead to arrange, deities to be bribed and appeased so that First Mother might be given a fair trial in the underworld by the black-faced Judge.

Yoke-lin watched Tua Kor and Tua Soh, the eldest daughter and the eldest daughter-in-law of the matriarch, giving directions to the other female members of the family about the arrangements for the household, while the matriarch's sons and sons-in-law took charge of the expenses for the wake and the funeral. As a daughter-in-law of the concubine, her status was low, so Yoke-lin remained on the fringe of these activities. Besides, she used to be a dance hostess and was also a relative newcomer to the family. In the three years since her marriage to Kim San, Yoke-lin had visited the Ong Mansion only three times: once during Soo Beng's First Moon and twice during the Lunar New Year.

So she sat quietly folding gilt joss papers into gold

bars and ingots as she listened to the talk of her sisters-in-law, trying to distinguish one from the other for they did not address one another by name. As in every large Chinese family, all the Ong brothers and sisters were addressed according to their order of birth, and so were their respective wives and husbands. Kim San, being son number six, was addressed as Sixth Brother by his siblings and their spouses, as Sixth Uncle by his nephews and nieces, or Lak Pek whenever they used the Hokkien dialect. His wife, Yoke-lin, became accordingly Sixth Sister-in-law or Lak Keem. Like many illiterate immigrants, the Ong patriarch and his wife invariably called their children Chicken, Dog or Cow, but as their brood expanded to a dozen or more with the children of the concubine and mistresses, the Ongs switched to the use of numerals as the easier way of remembering the birth order and identity of each child. None minded being a number, and like the rest, Yoke-lin was comfortable with this traditional hierarchy that gave each member of the family his or her rightful place.

"I was surprised, I tell you, that our old lady was so strong right up to the end. Always, ah, she said she'd outlive her old man. To claim his estate, ah, for her own children. Stubborn old lady, that one!" Second Sister-in-law uttered the sentiments which all the matriarch's daughters-in-law shared.

"When I first came into this household, ah," Second Sister-in-law continued, "many many quarrels between them! First Mother never accepted Father-in-law's women. She cried and cried! She brought him a dowry; that's how he became rich. When she couldn't control him, she offered him her bondmaid as concubine. Second Mother was twenty-five years younger. She gave birth to Sixth and Seventh Brothers. Aiyoh, First Mother used to scold her like a dog! At seventy or more, she was still jealous of the concubine!"

The matriarch's daughters-in-law sniggered.

"I hear the funeral and wake will cost close to forty thousand, all in," Fourth Sister-in-law complained, the worry lines on her forehead wrinkling at the thought of such a large sum towards which each sibling would have to contribute, especially the sons.

"Spending so much on the funeral, ah, when the gov'ment's going to take over our bus company is stupid, if you ask me," Third Sister-in-law said.

"Aiya, shhh, careful what you say. Walls have ears, ah, and if Tua Kor hears you, she'll come after you!" Fifth Sister-in-law muttered.

"Who cares? What I say here, I'll say to her face! You all are in such awe of her; I'm not! She it is who wants everything the same as Father-in-law's funeral! But things are different now! When this gov'ment takes over the company, ah, who will suffer? Not her husband! Ours! Where will the money come from?"

"Aiya, you know we can't bury First Mother in cheap wood," Fifth Sister-in-law said. "Everyone would talk behind our backs!"

"It's all this matter of face," Fourth Sister-in-law sighed. "What to do? I'll tell the children to cremate me when I die. Cheaper!"

Tua Kor came in with a troop of maidservants trailing her as she shouted directions in her shrill Hokkien.

"Ai! Ai! Put that wreath next to the altar! Second Aunt, ah, will think we look down on her if we put the wreath in the garden! What are you people doing? Sit and talk only!"

"Aiya, can't you see? We're folding joss papers. Shout only! You want help, all you have to do is open your mouth," Second Sister-in-law answered her back. She had always been more defiant than the rest, having come from a family of traders richer than the Ongs. "This here is Sixth Sister-in-law; ask her to help!"

Yoke-lin, knowing that she was a mere pawn in the

rivalry between the women, maintained a diplomatic silence throughout the exchange, neither accepting nor refusing the request for help. This earned her the silent approval of the other sisters-in-law, and eventually, they called to her, "Sixth Sister-in-law, come, help hold this for us." And she joined the group. But Yoke-lin knew that although everyone addressed everyone else by their rank and position in the family, it was not a sign of intimacy, no, not even friendliness sometimes. Such addresses were like grease that smoothened the formality and cordiality of familial relations, reminding each member that personal feelings aside, the person one disliked was a member of the family, and as the old folks preached, one's fingers should bend inwards into the palm and not stretch outwards towards strangers.

When all the gold and silver joss papers had been neatly folded and packed into paper chests, Yoke-lin escaped into the garden where workmen were putting up a huge green marquee of tarpaulin. Many hundreds of people were expected to come and pay their last respects to the matriarch of Ong Trading and Traction, not because they knew the old woman personally but because they had business dealings with the family conglomerate. Then there were the friends and relatives of the large Ong clan. Hundreds of chairs and tables were arranged under the marquee and the garden trees were strung with electric bulbs. An anticipation of festivity hung in the air as the servants covered the tables with white cloths and placed dishes of colourful sweets, fruits and melon seeds, and bottles of soft drinks on each table, for Tua Kor had insisted that everything must be done properly to look good.

Image and appearance count in the world of business and social relations, and Yoke-lin was convinced that what Tua Kor was doing would eventually benefit everyone in the family. She had pointed this out to Kim San again and again whenever he grumbled about the unnecessary expenses. Fifth Sister-in-law had also railed about the waste of money, but even she knew that it would not be good for her husband if people thought the Ongs were in financial trouble.

Secretly, Yoke-lin was pleased that Tua Kor's will had prevailed, and she could show friends like Yee Soh and Angela the pomp and ceremony attending a death in the Ong family.

Two thousand packets of soft drinks and a hundred crates of liquor and beer had been ordered, and the mansion's garage was stacked high with ice boxes. First and Second Aunts were supervising the dinners and suppers which would be served to all visitors during the three-day wake. Elaborate five-course dinners and simple tim-sum suppers of steamed buns and dumplings for hordes of acquaintances, business associates and relatives were already being prepared by the chefs of a Chinese restaurant. According to tradition, no visitor should leave a wake hungry. "A belly that's full gives a sense of plenty, and this will augur well for First Mother's descendants," the family's great grand uncle had pronounced in his ponderous Hokkien when the Ong siblings were bickering over the number of courses and dinners to serve during the wake. To offset bad luck, a thousand black cloth umbrellas and white paper fans and yards of red thread would be distributed to all mourners and friends at the funeral.

In the large sitting room of the mansion, a grand altar had been set up. Covered with blue and white satin on which were embossed black Chinese characters, it was dominated by a large black and white photograph of First Mother. On either side of her teakwood coffin was a life-size paper servant. The paper valet on the left served a packet of Dunhill cigarettes on a paper tray, not that the matriarch had ever smoked during her life, but the expensive brand, like her teakwood coffin, were indicative of wealth. The paper maid on the right of the coffin presented onlookers with a paper cup of coffee and a paper smile. The matriarch would be well-looked after in the next world. A paper mansion, costing five thousand dollars, filled with paper cut-outs of miniature furniture, a large paper ship and a paper Mercedes-Benz, the size of a couch, as well as paper chests filled with paper gold would be burnt for the financial security of the matriarch in the next world. Paper on paper, millions could be burnt, inherited and lost, this world being a reflection of the next in the eyes of the Ong clan.

A Chinese priest from the temple was chanting, in the Hokkien dialect, prayers to guide the matriarch's soul, persuading her gently to leave this world for the next.

"Empty is the valley of tears,
All is waste, all is nothing;
Chase not the evanescent,
Clutch not the shadows of life.

The blossoms bloom each spring
And wither each winter,
All paths lead to death.
Into this world you bring nothing,
Out of this world you take naught."

The irony of the chant in the midst of such opulence and ostentation was lost on Yoke-lin as she wiped away a tear at the thought of her own mother's tragic death. There had been no bands of musicians to drive away the devils, no banners and no wreaths. A lorry had transported the simple coffin and the family to the cemetery, where four men had lowered the coffin into a hole and covered it with earth. A week later, the trishaw rider, her step-father, had sold off all her sisters to a brothel keeper. She, Yoke-lin, had been fortunate to escape such a fate when Tai Ku came and took her away. It was fate, was it not? How else could she explain why Tai Ku, who had never seen her, should choose her instead of one of her sisters.

Only fate could explain the varied fortunes and destinies of man. Tai Shook, the butcher, remained a butcher all his life. But Ong Choon Teck, the bicycle repairer, became a millionaire. And yet both were illiterate immigrants who worked hard. Native talent alone could not account for one man's good fortune and another's perpetual poverty.

Yoke-lin wandered into other parts of the mansion. From the dining room came the chatter of children and the servants coaxing their charges to finish their meals so that the adults could have their turn. To the right of the passageway, a broad stairway with a carved balustrade led to the sleeping chambers upstairs. To the left were another row of rooms and two low worn steps that led through a glass door into the courtyard, paved with large square flagstones. Pots of lime bushes, pomelo and several kinds of large cacti believed to ward off evil were placed along the sides by the walls. The kitchen across the courtyard was next to the servants' quarters.

The solidity of the mansion, with its thick walls, ornate tiles, colonnades, portico and carved cornices, awed Yoke-lin with its sense of family history, as did the rosewood furniture with inlaid mother-of-pearl, and the odd pieces of imitation Italian marble figurines of the eighteenth century. She longed for a niche among these bric-a-brac. Stealthily, she stroked the semi-nude figurines but first making sure that no one was watching, and then she sat on the rosewood armchair that had been a favourite of her late father-in-law.

Crossing the courtyard, she entered the deserted kitchen. A rusty iron wok sat on the ancient brick stove in forgotten splendour. In recent years family feasts had been few and far between. When the patriarch was alive, anyone with the surname of Ong could come to the mansion for a free meal. During their courting days, Kim San used to recall those wonderful times, filling her head with stories of elaborate New Year celebrations and days of sumptuous feasting. But the tradition of communal hospitality had passed with the old man. Sibling rivalry and personal greed had sapped the common weal so that the family mansion had fallen into a state of slow decay, not for lack of money for repairs but for lack of unity. Each son and daughter had moved out of the mansion into houses of their own.

She caught sight of Second Mother, old and very wrinkled, seated at the kitchen table, absorbed in attacking a piece of chicken with the quick bites of a ravenous dog, pulling at the meat with her few remaining teeth. She was grotesque. Yoke-lin, who had met the old lady only once, was amazed. How could the concubine in such a rich family eat like this? It was as if the old woman feared the food would be snatched out of her hands any minute.

She remembered her first visit when Kim San had presented her and Soo Beng to his two mothers. First Mother had given the boy a gold trinket and her a gold bracelet. Then Second Mother was called from the kitchen where she had been cooking with the servants. And she had stood by the doorway, hesitant and docile, waiting for First Mother to signal to her to come forward. Only then had Second Mother crept in, bowed and stooped, and she had presented her grandson with an inferior gold trinket. Yoke-lin remembered, too, how the old lady had tears in her eyes when Tua Kor allowed her to carry Soo Beng for a while. Then, all too quickly, she had been ordered back into the kitchen and Kim San had resumed his conversation with First Mother. Yoke-lin recalled being surprised that Kim San, after a brief greeting, had ignored his own mother. But Yoke-lin had supposed that it was more out of pain than indifference that had made her husband appear so unfilial.

Long ago Chinese concubines, given names like Melon and Pomegranate, were expected to bear abundant fruit but they were not allowed to bring up their own children. All children born into the household belonged, by custom and tradition, to the first wife.

"Pomegranate! Why are you here?" Tua Kor shrieked from the kitchen doorway, her eyes blazing with unconcealed annoyance. She ignored Yoke-lin's presence and turned her sharp bird-like face towards the women who had followed her. "You people, ah! Look! See for yourself! Don't say I ill-treat her the moment First Mother passes away! First Mother treated her like a sister. Even left ten thousand for her funeral expenses next time! But what does this bondmaid do? The ingrate! Hiding in here to gorge as if this were her last meal in this life!"

Tua Kor cursed her father's concubine, who was the same age as herself, but who in terms of family hierarchy was her elder. Tua Kor however had no respect for bondmaids and concubines. "My mother suffered because of her! When First Mother was alive, that Kim San never came to see her. What wrong had First Mother done him, you tell me? The wife she got for him was not a bad one. Not from the cabaret, but from a good family! But that Kim San didn't want her. He blamed First Mother. It's his own mother who spoilt him! Like father like son! All the women he found for himself, all came from bars and cabarets!"

Yoke-lin was stung to the quick but she remained silent, not daring to make a scene. Meanwhile, Second Mother continued to gnaw and chew, impervious to the sounds of fury around her.

"Look at her! Just look at her! Eating like a pig! Once a bondmaid always a bondmaid! How to respect her like this?"

"Tua Kor! Leave Second Mother alone! She's suffered enough looking after First Mother!" Tua Soh, the eldest daughter-in-law shouted from the courtyard.

"Ha! Now you tell me what to do? Where were you

and Tua Pek when mother died? She was waiting for you both! Where were you when she was ill? Who hugged their purses? It was I who hired a nurse! I, the married daughter! Not that I want everyone to know how good I am! But you force me to! I, who am married out of this family, paid all the doctor's bills!" Tua Kor shrieked.

"Aiya, Tua Kor," Second Sister-in-law entered the fray with a disparaging wave of her hand and a mocking smile, "Aiya, as if we don't know you're already well-paid for your troubles. Didn't First Mother appoint you madam director?"

Tua Kor lunged forward at her sister-in-law. But she missed her footing and fell in a heap on the kitchen floor, sobbing at the ingratitude of all around her. She wailed like a traditional mourner till her voice was cracked and hoarse.

"Aiya, our mother, open your eyes and ears!" she cried. "In life you were blind to their faults! In death, see into their hearts! See, see, they've no hearts! Did I take a cent from you? Aiya, why did you make me director? I didn't ask for it, and now people say this and that! Open your mouth, Mother, and let the heavens know who is right and who is wrong!"

The relatives crowded round to console her and told the sisters-in-law to keep their quarrels till after the funeral because First Mother's spirit must be allowed to depart in peace. They helped Tua Kor into the mansion.

"Mad, all mad!" Second Mother shouted after them.

"Worship the high and step on the low.
And all the children, they come and go,"

she sang and shook her head.

28

When calm was restored, all the Ong brothers and sisters and their spouses sat down to dinner. Tua Kor, having recovered from her bout of tears, with her eyes just a little red, sat at the main table with her husband on her right, and her eldest brother and his wife, Tua Pek and Tua Soh, on her left. Both sisters-in-law maintained a surface calm and cordiality in front of the men, who carried on as usual because the quarrel was the women's affair. Second Brother, Third Brother, Fourth Brother and their wives made up the rest of the party at the main table. Yoke-lin and Kim San sat with Fifth Brother, his wife, Third Sister who was unmarried, and his other sisters and their husbands, all dull traders and shopkeepers in their fifties and sixties.

"Come, let's eat. The priests from Dragon Hill Temple will be here soon," Tua Kor announced. She picked up her pair of chopsticks, pinched a piece of steamed chicken from the dish in the centre of the table, dipped it into the bowl of ginger sauce, and popped it into her mouth before anyone could say another word. Despite the family's wealth and her own marriage to a trader of means, Tua Kor could never quite rid herself of certain vulgar tricks whenever she ate, habits established in those early years of poverty when she had to fight with her siblings for choice pieces of scarce meat.

Yoke-lin, who had been watching from the next table, smiled to herself, and was conscious that she herself was eating slowly even daintily.

"How much, ah, are we paying these priests?" asked Second Brother, his mouth full of chicken.

"Aaah, let's see, two thousand a night, so it'll be six thousand in all," Tua Soh said.

"Wah! Those priests are making a lot of money," Fifth Sister-in-law, the only Christian in the family, murmured to her husband, and the others at the table nodded.

"Aiya, eat; don't talk so much," Fifth Brother waved away his wife's comment impatiently. "Priests in the temple and priests in the church, no difference! All got to eat rice!" He did not want to get into a religious war of words with Tua Kor. Yoke-lin had been told that First Mother had never approved of his marriage to a Christian but Fifth Brother liked to say that he had stood up for his beliefs, and now that First Mother had passed away, he declared that he would be baptised as soon as the mourning period was over.

"I've worked out the total cost of the funeral, ah, and it won't be more than forty thousand." Tua Kor's husband, the tea merchant, took up the little white teapot, filled his own and his wife's cup, and tilted his head slightly to inhale its hot fragrance. "Hmmm, good tea, good tea, Goddess of Mercy brand," he smiled and nodded to the company, casually dismissing all their unspoken questions about costs. He had always handled the family's financial matters at such times, and although the gossips claimed that he made a tidy sum for his troubles, none could say that he was not thorough and meticulous in carrying out his duties.

His wife meanwhile was keeping a sharp eye on the servants as they changed the plates and bowls, and brought in a large steamed fish, beautifully garnished with diced onions, red dates, black mushrooms and slices of yellow ginger. This was soon followed by a vegetarian dish of mock roast duck and roast pork made of soya bean skin, and so skilfully sliced and arranged in succulent pieces that they looked like real meat. This was served with a sweet and sour sauce, and so many different types of vegetables that the whole party pronounced themselves fully satisfied with this penitential dish, and Tua Kor beamed with pleasure because she was the one who had engaged the chef to cook the meals for the wake. She knew that the family liked to dine well, and besides, the quality of the meals served during this wake would show how much the family was willing and able to spend to honour their First Mother.

For the last dish, the servants brought in bowls of steaming lotus seed and longan soup, a sweet hot dessert. And as the party sipped and slurped, Tua Kor brought up the question of the family mansion and who should live in it now that First Mother had passed away and each brother had his own residence. Her voice was formal and neutral betraying none of her personal concern about expenditure and the division of the family estate. None of her brothers was likely to live here, she pointed out. The mansion badly needed repairs and these were costly. Perhaps, she said, they should consider selling the mansion and dividing up the proceeds or ploughing the whole sum back into the family business.

Everybody began to speak at once, and voices grew louder and louder as each brother or sister clamoured to be heard. Then someone asked, "What about Second Mother? Where's she going to live now?"

"Aiya, everybody knows," Tua Kor replied, "we all got to look after our own mothers! Can't expect others to do it!"

"Second Mother is growing senile," Fifth Sister-in-law ventured, looking round the table for the others' reaction.

"I know. That's why Third Sister is coming to live with me. She's unmarried, and if she stays here, she'll end up looking after other people's mother!" Tua Kor sniffed.

There was a brief pause while the rest of her siblings

pondered over her words. They sipped their tea and waited for Kim San and his younger brother to speak. Yoke-lin too was waiting to hear what her husband had to say.

Kim San's face was stiff and impassive like a mask, as though the years of suppressing his feelings in the face of constant insults had hardened his facial muscles. "My family will move in here after the funeral," he said, not looking at anyone in particular. "I will pay for all repairs as long as Second Mother is living in this house."

It was unexpected; no one, not even Yoke-lin, had expected Kim San to take over the mansion and all the costs of repair and maintenance which would certainly be very high for such a large mansion. A chastened mood reigned for a few minutes as the servants cleared away the bowls and brought in pots of freshly brewed tea. Tua Kor, who had been making callous remarks about abandoned mothers and unfilial sons, was suitably subdued when she spoke.

"As the eldest in the family, and if no one disagrees, I'd say this is the best solution. Tua Pek, the eldest son, should live here, but since he can't, Sixth Brother's suggestion is good. Then we'll have a proper home and altar for our Father and First Mother. We can install their memorial tablets here, and return every year to pay our respects, that is, if our Sixth Brother thinks it's all right."

Kim San had a faint smile on his lips as he nodded solemnly. Everyone stood up, glad that dinner was over and the troubling question about the mansion had been settled. Nobody had wanted to sell the mansion; it would have meant such a loss of face, announcing to the whole world that the Ongs could not afford to maintain their ancestral home and their parents' memorial tablets would be shunted to a common temple hall.

What a brilliant stroke, Yoke-lin thought, proud of the man she had married. She pushed aside all his failings for the time being to bask in the glory of his victory over his siblings, the children of his father's first wife. And he had done it in so few words! Such a contrast to Tua Kor's gabble. Now the children of First Mother would have to return to the mansion, not with the rights of residents, but only as relations invited home to pay their respects to their parents. And when they stepped into the mansion, they would have to pay their respects to their father's concubine and former bondmaid too. In time to come, Second Mother would be regarded by the other relatives as the matriarch and Kim San's family would acquire social importance and prestige as the main branch of the Ong family, because traditionally, those who lived in the family mansion always enjoyed a higher status than those living away from it.

Everyone had gathered around Kim San, eager to find out more about his business and how he could have come up with so much money for the repairs. Yoke-lin stood beside her husband, graciously accepting the congratulatory cluckings of her sisters-in-law. She was no longer just a newcomer, nor the daughter-in-law of a former bondmaid, but the wife of a successful trader. Later in life, she would tell her daughter, Yenti, that a woman must know how to suffer in silence beside her successful man, for the sake of his face, of family harmony and her children's well-being and education. And it was because she had known that all these things were at stake that she had chosen to turn a blind eye to his affairs and peccadilloes.

"Aiya, Sixth Sister-in-law, how lucky you are! I always said Kim San is filial ah! Don't think lowly of him, I said, and see, how true were my words!" Fourth Sister-in-law gushed.

Second Sister-in-law, who had hardly spoken more than three words to her, came forward too to ask after the children and to insist that she should bring Soo Beng to play with her son. Gratified, Yoke-lin stood beside her husband while he answered the family's queries, her mind already busy re-arranging the rosewood table and chairs, and deciding how she would dispose of those embarrassing

Italian figurines and replace them with the more dignified statuettes of Happiness, Prosperity and Longevity in long flowing Chinese robes.

Justice had been done, Yoke-lin felt, as in the Cantonese melodramas in which the downtrodden son of the bondmaid rose to become the new master of the mansion. And she, the downtrodden dance hostess, was its new mistress. All things were possible if one had the blessings of the Eight Immortals and Fate. She was more certain than ever now that her fate was linked to Kim San's and she would stand by him through rain or shine, eating porridge when there was only porridge and rice when there was rice. Busily, her mind wove a romance of rags-to-riches for an imaginary audience.

The gong sounded in the hall. The saffron-robed priests had arrived. Wearing once again its public face of unity, the family assembled in front of First Mother's altar. Yoke-lin spied her daughter standing awkwardly in a corner of the sitting room with Soo Beng in her arms. "Mama!" the boy called out. Yoke-lin's heart swelled with maternal pride at the sight of the son who had brought her such good fortune. Indeed, he was truly a gift from the gods!

"Yenti! Come over here!" she called out to her gawky teenage daughter, who still did not know how to dress to make herself attractive. "Bring Soo Beng here! Come stand next to Ah Pa!" She had raised her voice so that all in the room could hear her and see for themselves that Kim San treated his step-daughter as his own. And implicit in that gesture was the broad hint that nobody should look down upon the girl. Now that the mansion was going to be their home, Yoke-lin felt that they should stand with Kim San in the centre, and not at the fringe, shoulder to shoulder with the direct descendants of First Mother.

The five saffron-robed priests entered, chanting prayers, and everyone gathered round the altar in rows of white, black, and blue, with a sprinkling of green mourning outfits worn by the matriarch's great grandchildren. The colour of the mourning clothes defined the individual's relationship to the dead. The matriarch's sons and daughters-in-law, deemed the closest to her, donned white cotton and sack cloth; her daughters and sons-in-law wore black, but those with parents-in-law still living had to wear a patch of red on their right shoulders to make sure that Death would not follow them back to their matrimonial homes. All the grandchildren wore blue and in this way, by an intricate colour code, an individual's place in the family hierarchy is defined.

"Nam-mo-nam-mo-or-li-ah-tor!" the priests began the ritual with a Hokkien operatic chant, enticing the departed soul to return home for one last look at her beloved family before she crossed the River of Forgetfulness into the next world. Then the priests sang a Hokkien requiem tracing the soul's sorrowful journey through the Chinese Underworld.

"Cry, you all must cry loudly for First Grandmother," Tua Kor urged the matriarch's grandchildren. "You don't cry, ah, the guards down there will beat her and put her in chains!"

"Long ago, rich families even hired official mourners to cry at their funerals," Second Aunt explained. "The louder we cry, the less she'll be beaten, because then the Judge of Hell will know she did much good on earth, and that's why we cry for her."

A chair had been placed beside the altar and draped over it was a suit of the matriarch's samfoo jacket and trousers. On the floor was a pair of her shoes. Second Mother, old and wrinkled, was crouched beside the chair, burning joss papers, sheet by sheet, in the earthen pot, silently mourning her mistress who had given her, the bondmaid, a place and identity in the family. In her old heart there was no grudge, for all was but fate.

Smoke and incense thickened the air. The chief priest poured libations of wine and tea upon the floor, calling the spirit of the departed to return and see how her family was grieving for her. He beat the gong, giving the family the cue to cry.

"Ah Bu, ah, our Mother, don't say farewell yet!" Tua Kor, well-versed in such rituals, began. She was the chief mourner, her voice rising and falling with the cadence of a temple prayer.

"Don't leave us, your children, so quickly;
Look again at the faces of those you bore in your womb,
See the tears streaming from our eyes.
O, our long-suffering Mother,
Your life is a song of pain.
From youth to age, black hair to white,
In sickness and in health, you toil
Sunrise to sunset, day by day,
Through the withering years,
Your sons and daughters grinding you to the bone,
To the bone.
For what purpose was your toil?
For what gain was your suffering?"

Tua Kor's song of mourning reminded each son and daughter of their bond and debt to First Mother, bringing tears to their eyes. As they wept and listened to the chant, the family contemplated on the futility of their own lives, putting aside their personal grievances for the moment to mourn the loss of the mother who had borne them for nine months in her womb. And Yoke-lin, recalling how she had been called to the old woman's bedside, wept with them, holding little Soo Beng, her gift from the gods, in her arms.

Yenti's Journal

There! I've finished!

I have buried my family, given each one his due, and in the process, freed myself of the ghosts which haunt the mind. This writing is an act of remembrance as well as a severance of the ties that bound me to what I was. From now on I shall sculpt a new me!